MW00612539

THE GIANT KILLER

KILLER

OR THE BATTLE WHICH ALL MUST FIGHT

TIMELESS CHRISTIAN CLASSICS
from GENERATIONS

Heidi

The Holy War

The Pilgrim's Progress for Young Readers

Robinson Crusoe

The Swiss Family Robinson

Titus: A Comrade of the Cross

The Life of Henry Martyn

The Dragon and the Raven

Sunshine Country

The Princess Bellaheld

The Giant Killer

Mary Jones and Her Bible

THE GIANT KILLER

KILLER

OR THE BATTLE WHICH WE ALL MUST FIGHT

Charlotte Maria Tucker

(A.L.O.E.)

Contents

The Readings

CHAPTER 1

THE ARRIVAL

Well, I hope that we're near the end of our journey at last!" exclaimed Adolphus Probyn, with a long weary yawn, as the Fly which was conveying him and his brother from the station rolled slowly along a quiet country road.

"You're in a precious hurry to get there," said Constantine, fixing his thumbs in his waistcoat pockets, and putting up his feet on the opposite seat; "but I don't believe that you'll like the place when you see it. I hate being sent to a private tutor's; I'd rather have gone to a regular school at once."

"I don't know as that," said Adolphus, who had some vague ideas in his mind about fagging, hard dumplings, and wooden benches.

"One thing I know," cried his brother, "I'm certain to dislike this tutor with all my heart."

Adolphus did not take the trouble to ask his reasons, but Constantine went on without stopping to be questioned.

"I should dislike any one recommended by Aunt Lawrence, she's so particular, thinks so many things wrong, is so fond of good books and lectures, and that sort of thing. Depend upon it, she put into papa's head that we were spoilt, and needed someone to keep us in order, and she found out this poor country clergyman"—

"Poor—I'm sorry he's poor," observed Adolphus; "he'll not make us half so comfortable as we were at home. I wonder if he'll have no late second dinner."

"Oh, you may make up your mind to that!" cried his brother; "all the family will dine together at One on boiled mutton and rice pudding, or bacon and beans!"

Adolphus sighed. "And it will be work, work, work, from morning till night, with no change but long sermons, long lectures, and long walks; and if we go bird nesting, or have a little fun, won't we catch it,—that's all!"

"Here we are at last!" said Adolphus, as the fly stopped at a little green door.

The Finish of the Journey

Constantine put his head out the window. "No carriage drive," he muttered; "what a mean place it must be!"

Scarcely had the coachman's pull at the bell broken the peaceful stillness of that quiet spot, when the green door was thrown wide open, and a boy of about eleven years of age appeared at it, with a broad smile of welcome on his face.

"I'm so glad you've come—we've been waiting dinner for you; let me help down with that," he added, as the coachman made preparations for lifting down a black trunk which had kept him company on the box.

Constantine jumped from the carriage; his twin brother more slowly descended, and without troubling themselves with their luggage, or taking much notice of their new companion, they proceeded along the narrow gravel-walk which led up to the entrance of the dwelling.

A pretty cottage it appeared, though a small one, with the sunshine gleaming through the twining roses on the diamond-panelled windows, that peeped from beneath the low thatched roof. It would have looked very well in a picture; not a chimney but was twisted into some elegant shape; the whole building, nestling in trees and garlanded with creepers, might have served as a model to a painter. But as Adolphus gazed curiously upon his new home, it looked to his eye rather too much like a magnified toy: he began to wonder to himself where room could be found in it for him and his brother, especially when he saw two little girls standing in the porch watching their arrival with a look of shy pleasure.

Boys of ten years of age are, however, seldom long troubled with thoughts such as these, and the attention of young Probyn was almost immediately diverted by the appearance of Mr. and Mrs. Roby, who advanced to welcome their guests to Dove's Nest. The former was a tall, pale gentleman, with

The Reception

a stoop, a high forehead and thoughtful air, which at once impressed the two little boys with an idea that a very learned scholar was before them. Mrs. Roby, on the contrary, was stout and rather short, with a bright merry glance in her dark eyes, to which the dimples in her cheeks corresponded; there was kindliness in the press of her hand, and a cheerful animation about her whole manner that made her guests feel at home with her at once.

"I see that my Aleck has introduced himself to you already," said she, smiling, "but here are other little friends glad to see you, and anxious, I am sure, to make you happy. Bertha—Laura—my darling," she continued, laying her hand fondly on the curly head of the youngest child, the little image of herself, with her bright eyes and merry glance, "you should bid these young gentlemen welcome."

The Probyns were soon shown to the room which they

were to share with Aleck; and though the ceiling was low, and sloped down on one side, and the single window was certainly small, he would have been difficult to please indeed, who could have found fault with so pretty an apartment. Everything was so beautifully clean and neat, and through that open window came so sweet an air; while the tinkle of a distant sheep-bell, and the carol of birds from the neighbouring trees, made music delightful after the rattle of a railway, or the ceaseless roll of carriages in London.

The dinner, also, to which the Probyns speedily descended, was excellent, though simple; and Adolphus especially, who had soon managed to find out that no second one was to be expected, did ample justice to the good cheer after his long journey, having quite forgotten sundry parcels of sandwiches and cake which he had managed to dispose of by the way. Being rather shy at first, and under the eye of Mr. Roby, the boys were upon their good behaviour, and everything went on very harmoniously. Laura had indeed to squeeze up very close to her mother to avoid the elbows of Constantine, and opened her merry eyes wider than usual when Adolphus, seeing that the plum tart was rapidly disappearing, thrust forward his plate for a second help before he had half finished his first. But no open notice was taken of either breach of good manners; this was not the time to find fault. Mr. Roby sat quiet and observant, and his two little daughters said little; but their mother led the conversation, in which Aleck joined freely, and before the dinner was over the Probyns were quite at their ease.

"We shall have plenty of things to show you," said Aleck; "papa has given us all a half-holiday in honour of your arrival. There are my two rabbits, the black and the white one."

"I like rabbit curry very much," interrupted Adolphus.

"Oh, but you are not to eat them!" exclaimed little Laura in alarm, shocked at the idea of cooking her favourites.

"And there is the garden," continued Aleck; "We have made two arches across the gravel-walk, and such beautiful creepers are twined round them; and there is a famous bower at the end of it—we helped to pave it with pebbles ourselves."

"And there's a cow!" cried Laura; "you shall see her milked!"

"Then we will have some syllabub, that we will!" exclaimed Adolphus.

The little Robys looked at each other, and then glanced at their mother, in astonishment at such a bold and unusual proposal. The lady, somewhat to their surprise, gave a smiling consent, and poured out nearly a tumbler-full of home-made wine in preparation for this unwonted treat.

"This is not so bad," thought Constantine; "I daresay we'll have some fun here. I shall like to tease that prim puss Miss Bertha a little, who looks as though she considered it wrong to open her mouth; and we'll bring down Master Aleck a peg or two - he thinks himself mighty clever, I can see."

"This is a great deal better than school," —such were the reflections of Adolphus. "The master looks mild enough, the lady is the picture of good-nature, and these people don't appear to be shabby, although they are certainly poor."

Yes, Mr. Roby was poor; even had his income been double what it was, one so generous and benevolent would still have been poor. He could not afford to give Aleck, his only son, the advantage of a school, but this seemed no misfortune to the affectionate father; he preferred conducting his boy's education himself. Aleck was naturally clever, and, under the careful training of his parent, had made uncommon progress in his studies. If there was anything on earth of which the clergyman was proud, it was the talents and goodness of his son.

Quiet and reserved as Mr. Roby was, it was no small trial to him to introduce strangers into his peaceful home, though these strangers were the nephews of an intimate friend; it

Helping at Lessons

was a sacrifice of inclination to duty. But his wife, in encouraging him to make this sacrifice, had other reasons beyond increasing their small means, or obliging the aunt of the Probyns. Mrs. Roby, with her clear common sense, saw that it was not good for her Aleck to have no companion but his sisters. They were both younger than himself, and looked up to him in everything. He helped them in their lessons, took the lead in their amusements, and was loved by them with the fondest affection. What wonder if the boy was becoming a little spoiled; he was of too much importance in the quiet home-circle; he could not but feel that his parents were proud of him—that his sisters regarded him as one who could scarcely do wrong; he grew too fond of giving his opinion—too self-confident, and his mother saw it. Hers was, however, the eye of partial affection, and she had little idea how often those who had been gratifying her husband by praising the uncommon talents and virtues of their son, behind his back spoke of him as "a conceited boy, who loved to hear himself talk, who was ruined by being brought up at home, and would never be good for anything in the world."

Oh, how startled should we often be, could we know the difference between what is said to us, and what is said of us; what a shock would our vanity receive, could we look beyond the smile of flatterers and see into their hearts!

CHAPTER 2

FIRST IMPRESSIONS

The next morning Aleck and his sisters met their mother in the breakfast-parlour before their guests had left their sleeping apartment. Mr. Roby was still engaged in his study, having as usual risen at five, that he might not leave one of his various duties neglected.

"Mamma," said Bertha, after having received her morning's kiss, "I am afraid that we shall not like these Probyns at all."

"It is too early to decide upon their characters," replied Mrs. Roby; "we must wait till we know them a little better."

"I think Constantine a very disagreeable boy," said Bertha; "he has a sort of—I don't know what sort of manner, but it is not in the least like Aleck's. It is as though he despised us for being girls; and he kicks his feet against the legs of the table, and never keeps still for a moment, and it fidgets

15

me so—I can't bear it!" The little girl's brow was all wrinkled over with frowns.

"And he's so naughty," said Laura, resting her arms on her mother's knee, and looking up gravely into her face. "He pulled the cow's tail, and would not leave off, and when we told him that it hurt her, he only laughed!"

"You should have seen how the boys quarrelled for the syllabub," continued Bertha, "pulling and struggling till half of it was thrown over between them."

"And they never let me have one drop," added Laura; "I think that they are shocking bad boys!"

"So they are," said Aleck, as he paused in his task of cutting the loaf for breakfast; "they never read their Bibles before going to bed, nor said their prayers neither, as far as I could tell." Aleck did not add—indeed, he did not consider, that although he himself had not omitted to kneel down, as he had been taught from his childhood to do, his thoughts had been so much taken up with his new companions, and drawing a contrast between their conduct and his own, that not a feeling of real devotion had given life to his heartless prayer.

"Not say their prayers!" cried Laura, looking more shocked than before; "did you ever think that there were such wicked boys?"

"And such stupid ones too," rejoined Aleck. "When I spoke to them about their lessons, Adolphus said, with a great yawn, that learning was a bore." Laura raised her eyebrows with an expression of arch surprise. "I offered to lend him my account of the famous Cook. 'Oh, I know all about him already,' said he; 'his name was Soyer, and he made a capital sauce!'" Here two merry dimples appeared on the little child's cheeks, and deepened as her brother proceeded:

"And when I asked him if he did not like Caesar, he thought that I was speaking of a dog, and inquired if he was one that would not bite!"

This overcame Laura's gravity altogether; she burst into such a merry ringing laugh that neither Bertha nor Aleck could help joining her heartily; and even Mrs. Roby, who was meditating a little lecture to her children on too hastily judging others, found it difficult to keep her countenance.

The entrance of the Probyns stopped the mirth of which they had been the subject. Breakfast passed over; then came hours of study, which served to strengthen Aleck in his opinion that his companions were very stupid boys. Adolphus appeared the dullest of the two; not that he naturally was so, but he had always been too lazy to learn. He stumbled at every word in his reading, spelt *pheasant* with an f, and *thumb* without a b, could not see any difference between a noun and a verb, and confused the Red Sea with the Black. Poor Mr. Roby, accustomed to an intelligent pupil, stifled a quiet sigh; and Aleck, with a feeling of vast superiority, could not hide the mingled surprise, amusement, and contempt, which the boy's ignorance called up in his own mind. The Probyns noticed the smile on his face, and it stung them more than a real injury would have done; while indulging his secret pride, Aleck was sowing in the hearts of his companions bitter feelings of resentment and hate.

After lessons, an hour was given to play in the garden; but anything but play it proved to Aleck, for the Probyns were determined to show him that, if he had more book-learning than they, he, a country boy, was ignorant of many things familiar to them from living in London. Without coming to an open quarrel, they made him feel that they disliked him, showed such open contempt for what he valued, and treated his favourite pursuits with such scorn, that, irritated almost beyond his power of endurance by a trial to which he was unaccustomed, Aleck lost both his patience and his temper, and was laughed at for being so easily "put in a pet." It was fortunate for him that the time had now come for joining his mother and sisters in the parlour. The boys found the little ladies busy at their sewing; Mrs. Roby had quitted the room to see a poor woman who had come for advice and assistance.

"This is our nice half-hour with mamma," said Laura; "she always reads something to us before dinner while we work, and Aleck draws beside her."

"More reading!" exclaimed Adolphus, with no pleased look.

"Oh, but it's amusing reading!" said Laura. "There, Aleck dear, I've put your copy and pencil all ready for you; and I've not forgotten the India-rubber this morning, you see, though I am such a careless little thing!" Another time she would have been repaid by a smile and a kiss; but Aleck was in no mood for that now.

"Amusing reading! I wonder what you call amusing!" said Constantine, who, to Bertha's great annoyance, was occupying his idle fingers in turning over the contents of her work-box.

"Why, mamma has been reading to us little bits," said Laura ; " only little bits such as I can understand, you know, of the history of good Mr. Budgett, the 'Successful Merchant.'"

"The Successful Merchant! I'll not stand that!" exclaimed Constantine, flinging Bertha's reels of cotton right and left, as she threw himself back in his chair.

"Oh, but it's so curious—so interesting—and all true! There's the story of the little donkey, and of the horse that was lost, and the great tea-party—things that amuse even me."

"Amuse a stupid girl like you; but"—

"If you talk about stupidity," cried Aleck, firing up, "let me tell you"—

Oh, how thankful the girls were for the entrance of their mother at this moment! To see flushed faces, fiery looks, clenched fists, was so new to them, that, in terror lest their darling brother should be drawn into a quarrel and be hurt, poor little Laura could scarcely restrain her tears, and Bertha, as she stooped to pick up her reels, wished from her heart that these odious new-comers had never arrived to break the peaceful serenity of Dove's Nest.

Mrs. Roby's quick eye instantly detected that there had been words amongst the children; she thought it best, however, to take no notice of this, and opening a little drawer in her table, took out of it a manuscript book.

"I have been thinking what kind of reading might serve to entertain you all, uniting some instruction with amusement." Constantine turned down his lips at the word instruction. He thought that the lady did not see him. "Here is an allegory—a sort of tale which contains a hidden meaning beneath the apparent one—and"—

"But I don't like hearing reading, ma'am," interrupted Adolphus, with much more candour than good manners.

"No kind of reading?" inquired Mrs. Roby, in perfect good-humour.

"I think, then, that this book may suit your taste; it is the story of a Giant-killer."

"Oh, some story-books, and fairy-tales, I don't mind them, if I've nothing better to amuse me."

"Jack the Giant-killer! Oh, I've heard that a thousand times!" cried Adolphus, while the Robys could scarcely help laughing at the idea of their mother reading such a story to them.

"Mine is a new Giant-killer—a great hero, I can assure you," said the lady; "and I think that my tale is a better one than that with which you are so well acquainted, as it contains a great deal that is true."

"Why, there are no giants now!" cried Constantine.

"I am not so sure of that," replied Mrs. Roby; "I believe that we might find both giants and giant-killers in the world at this time, if we only knew where to look for them."

"I should like to hear this story," said Constantine, afraid of the lady's returning to the "Successful Merchant."

Winding the Skein

"Then perhaps you would kindly wind this skein of silk for me while I read," said Mrs. Roby, willing to save an unfortunate tidy from the fingers which were now picking at its fringe. "There, let me find the end for you. I am sure that Adolphus will oblige me by turning the skein while you wind; and, now that you are all busily employed, I will at once begin my little book."

CHAPTER 3

GIANT SLOTH

It was the still hour of twilight. The moon still shone in the deep blue sky; but her light was becoming pale and dim. The stars had gone out, one by one, and a red flush in the east, deepening into crimson just behind the hill, showed where the sun would shortly appear.

A knight lay stretched on the mossy ground; his head reclined on a shield, his two-handed sword girt to his side— even in sleep his hand rested on the hilt. This was the brave champion Fides, the chosen knight to whom had been given mighty treasures and a golden crown by the King whom he had served from his childhood. But he was not yet to enter into possession of his riches, he was not yet to wear his bright crown; hard labours, great dangers were before him—he was to fight before he might enjoy. So Fides was to pass alone through the enemy's land, to slay every giant who should oppose him on the way. His King had provided him with strong armour, and with a wondrous sword which gave certain victory if he who drew it shrank not back like a coward, or yielded to the foe like a traitor; he had, in truth, nothing to fear but his own slackness in fight; if but faithful, he must be triumphant.

The knight slept soundly on his soft couch, for he was weary with long travel that night. He was roused by the touch of a hand, so light that the dew could hardly have rested more gently on his shoulder; and yet there was something in the power of that touch which not only broke his slumbers, but restored to him in a moment all his waking powers. He started up, and beheld before him a beautiful messenger sent by his King. Her robe was of woven light, a starry crown was upon her head, and the glance of her eye penetrated the heart, and laid open its most in most feelings. Fides recognized Conscience, his companion and friend, who, invisible to all eyes but his own, had come on an errand to the knight.

"Sleeping still!" she exclaimed, "with your labours all to come—sleeping on the enemy's ground! Rouse you, recreant champion, and draw your sword; see you not yon towers before you? It is there that Giant Sloth holds his court; you cannot pass on until he is slain. This is the hour to attack him in his hold; soon after sunrise he quits it to roam abroad; if not attacked early, he will escape your pursuit;—on, then, and victory attend you!"

"O Conscience, I am weary!" Fides replied; "a little more rest may be mine! The sun is scarcely seen above yon ridge; grant me another hour's slumber."

"Go at once," replied the bright one, "or you go in vain."

"But how make my way into the castle?"

"Press the hilt of your sword against the heaviest door, and it will open as if by a key."

"But if difficulties should arise, or doubts perplex me."

Knight Fides and Conscience

"Breathe upon the hilt of your sword, and you will behold me beside you. Though unseen, I will ever be near you. Delay not now, for, look at the sun, what a flood of light he pours on the world! When the great clock in the giant's tower strikes six, it will be too late to encounter him that day; he may vanish before your eyes, but neither be conquered nor slain. Go!" And even as the words were upon her lips, the bright one vanished from his sight.

With rapid step and a resolute spirit, Fides sped on to his first encounter. The way was plain before him; not even the youngest child could have mistaken it. In front arose the castle of Giant Sloth, whose heavy, shapeless mass looked as though it had been built of clouds. Fides, sword in hand, pressed up to the door; it was open, as if to invite his entrance, and heat once proceeded into the large hall.

A strange scene of confusion was there; the whole place was littered with unfinished work, blotted pages and blank ones, play-books torn and without their backs, dresses in rags, and neglected volumes with leaves yet uncut. But the strangest thing was the feeling of heaviness and dullness which stole over the knight the moment that he entered the hall. It seemed too much trouble even to pass through its length; he would fain have laid himself down and slept. The place was very still, the only sound heard was that of some one heavily breathing in a room that was near; Fides doubted not that this was the giant himself.

Animated with the hope of gaining his first triumph, the knight resolutely struggled against the sleepy sensation which made the danger of that enchanted hall. He passed through it, and found at the end that what he at a distance had mistaken for a wall, was only a huge web, like that which the house-spider weaves; not the light net-work which is strung with bright beads of dew, but thick, close, and darkened with dust. Through this strange curtain Fides with some difficulty could see into the inner room where the giant lay asleep.

Sloth's huge, clumsy form was half sunk in a great heap of down, not a feather of which stirred in the heavy air, except such as were moved by his breathing. Here, then, was the knight, and there was his foe, but how was the first to reach the latter! Only the web was between, and Fides threw his whole weight against it, hoping easily thus to get through; not so, it bent, but it did not break—every thread in the yielding curtain seemed as strong as though it had been made of iron wire.

Fides drew back disappointed and surprised; something that was not weariness, but possessed the same power to deaden energy and make effort disagreeable, seemed pressing his spirit down. His eyelids grew heavy, he could scarcely keep them open, he felt a strong and increasing desire to indulge the sleepiness which had now come over him. But there was an object before him which made him struggle against the enchantment. Just above the feathery couch of the giant was a huge clock, with a dial of silver and numbers of gold, and the hand, which glittered with many a gem, had almost touched the point of six.

"Now or never!" thought Fides, with another strong effort, as he remembered the words of Conscience. Again the web yielded to his weight, but not the smallest flaw appeared in its fine texture to give him hope of succeeding in breaking through.

"Ding-ding-ding!" the hand is at six—the giant is beginning to stir! Fides with sudden resolution lifts his sword on high, down it descends on the web, which, as the blow divides it, starts back on each side till a very wide gap appears. Fides springs through the opening, he is just in time, and the next moment Giant Sloth lies dead at his feet.

"Well," exclaimed Adolphus, with a comical expression on his face, as soon as Mrs. Roby had closed her book, "I suspect that this story, from beginning to end, is all a hit upon me."

"I thought that it was a hit upon me," said little Laura," when I heard of the broken-backed play-books, and the room in such shocking disorder!"

"It might have been a hit upon me," thought Bertha, who,

Fides Slays the Giant Sloth

indolent by disposition, had felt the moral touch her in the description of unfinished work.

"It is a hit upon no one," replied Mrs. Roby, "unless any person present chooses to consider himself as Giant Sloth or one of his brotherhood. Your faults are your enemies, the greatest enemies of those over whom they exercise the greatest power. Pray, at this our first reading of 'the Giant-killer,' let me impress this strongly upon your minds. I would not

hurt the feelings of one of my listeners, far less would I encourage them to find out and laugh at the follies of each
other. My desire is to lead you to consider that you are all
and each of you yourselves in the position of my hero. The
foes which he had to conquer you also must fight; you have
the same aid to encourage you, the same motives to rouse.
The same giant may not be equally formidable to you all, but
everyone has some enemy with whom he must struggle, in a
strength that is given to him, armour not his own."

"Ah!" said Aleck, "I was sure that there was some meaning
in that part of the story. The two-handed sword also, which
nothing could resist"—

"What was that?" interrupted Constantine.

"I would rather that you should discover that for yourself," said Mrs. Roby. "If the kernel of an allegory be good, it
is worth the trouble of cracking the shell."

"Oh, but I hate all trouble!" cried Adolphus; "above all,
the trouble of thinking."

"Take care, take care," laughed little Laura, "or we shall
suspect that you have been caught by Giant Sloth."

CHAPTER 4

GIANT SELFISHNESS

D o you know, mamma," said Laura the next day, as she and her sister sat alone with their mother, the boys being at lessons in the study—"do you know that I did not feel inclined to get up when I was called; but the clock began to strike, which put Giant Sloth into my head, and up I jumped in a minute!"

"I am glad that you made such practical use of my little tale," replied Mrs. Roby, with a smile.

"But, mamma—if I might say something," began Bertha, then hesitated and paused.

"Say anything that you please, my dear."

"I almost wondered at your beginning with only Giant Sloth; that seems such a little fault compared with the great ones of the Probyns. Constantine did not seem hit at all, for he is active enough in mischief."

"I repeat that I hit no one," replied her mother.

"Oh!—but—you know what I mean, mamma; I should have liked something very—very"—Bertha's face had a puzzled look, for she knew not how to express her meaning; "I should have liked some story that would have made them know themselves, and hate their faults as everyone else must hate them. I would have had a horrible Giant Selfishness!" she added, her manner becoming more excited as she spoke.

"You look upon selfishness, then, as their grand enemy!"

"Oh, mamma, can anything be plainer—they are made up of selfishness, nothing but selfishness; they never think of the comfort of any one. I am sure that I wish they had never come here, to torment us!" her cheek flushed, and her eye filled as she spoke.

"Come, come, my love, if you are so warm on the subject, I shall suspect that the poor Probyns are not the only ones here who feel the power of Giant Selfishness."

"Mamma! What do you mean?" said Bertha, in surprise.

"I believe I am convinced that you would suffer far less from the conduct of these boys if there were not something in your own nature of the same quality which you so strongly condemn in them."

"I never thought that you would have accused me of selfishness!" said Bertha, with a good deal more sullenness in her tone than might have been expected from a child so well brought up.

"What makes you feel so extremely annoyed when your pleasures are interfered with, your little amusements interrupted, your time broken in upon, your things wanted for others?"

"No one likes to be put out of their way," replied Bertha.

"No one likes it, my love, and selfishness is a quality to

Bertha and Her Mother

which, I fear, very few indeed are strangers."

"My brother and sister do not think me selfish—I would do anything for them."

"You love them, and love makes all things easy; besides that, it seems to me that they seldom put your self-denial to any great trial. To attend your brother, to work for him, to carry out his little plans, has been your greatest amusement; and as for Laura"—the child had just left the room to bring her forgotten spelling book—"she is such a sweet-tempered little creature that there could be no merit in showing kindness to her."

"Then why are these boys brought here to make me selfish when I was not so before?" cried Bertha, with bitter emotion. "They seem to have brought all sorts of evil with them—even Aleck does not appear the same that he was—he is not half so much with his sisters; they are filling my heart with such angry feelings—I shall never be good while they are here."

"They are teaching you *to know yourself*, my Bertha; they

are not causing the selfishness in your soul, they are only tearing away the veil which prevented you from knowing that it was there. A gilt object may appear as well as a gold one until it is tried in the fire, it is the furnace of temptation which proves of what metal we are made. A lake looks clear and pure while perfectly still; the oar which stirs up the sand from below is not the cause of the sand being there, it lay in the depths before, like evil in the depths of our hearts."

Bertha heaved a deep sigh. "It is very painful to find out that we are so much worse than we thought ourselves," she said.

"The discovery is painful, but very valuable. You would not go to meet an enemy blindfold; *you must see him before you can fight him*, you must know your faults before you can subdue them."

Bertha felt the truth of her mother's words, and instead of only dwelling on the failings of their guests, she applied the lesson to herself, when her mother read to the assembled children the story of

Giant Selfishness

Giant Selfishness sat in his bower, which was all garlanded over with flowers. The honeysuckle twined round its slender pillars; damask roses and white, tinged with a pale blush, clambered over the roof; while around a marble basin, from which a bright fountain tossed its sparkling waters in the sun, the geranium scattered its delicate blossoms, and the fuchsia shook its crimson tassels in the breeze. A fair bower it was, for it had been adorned by Pleasure, the willing servant and attendant on its lord.

Giant Selfishness was huge of stature and strong of limb;

taller and more powerful than his younger brother, Sloth. There were few indeed who could cope with his arm, he was tyrant over half the world. Many a great conqueror he had made his slave, thousands and thousands had felt his chains, he claimed dominion over young and old. Yet now, as the giant sat alone, a deep shade of gloom was upon his massive brow; he listened not to the tinkling fall of the fountain, he glanced not at the beautiful flowers. "Evil tidings, evil tidings!" he muttered to himself; "Sloth has been the first victim, but he will not be the last. I dread nothing on earth but the invincible sword; not even my strength can stand against that!" He pressed his vast hand over his eyes, and remained for some moments in thought.

"Ha! I have it!" he exclaimed, suddenly raising his head; "what force cannot accomplish, cunning may perform." He clapped his hands as a signal, and the noise that they made was startling as a peal of thunder.

Instant at the summons his servant Pleasure appeared.

A fairy-like creature, with gossamer wings, all sparkling with the tints of the rainbow.

"Pleasure," exclaimed the giant, "I call thee to my aid against him who would root out the race of Selfishness. Knowest thou if Fides is still at the castle where Sloth this morning fell beneath his sword?"

"He is still there," replied the musical voice of Pleasure; "he finds much to arrange, and much to do, but will leave ere the sun goes down."

"He must not leave it till the night dew falls!" cried the giant, leaning forward on his seat, and speaking in a low, earnest tone. "Hie thou to yon castle, Pleasure; spread there for him a table that may lure him to delay; load it with rich wines and the daintiest food; make it tempting, as thou

35

Giant Selfishness Instructing Pleasure

knowest how to make it."

Pleasure had learned many a recipe from old Gluttony her neighbour, and, confident in her own powers, only answered the giant by a smile.

"There is no moon to-night," continued Selfishness; "if he tarry till dark, he is my prey. Then when he sets forth from Castle Sloth, do thou, with a lantern in thine hand, dance before him like the wild-fire on the waste; draw him from the path which he should pursue, lead him on to the deep pit in the woods which I have dug to catch wanderers like him."

Pleasure bowed as she received the command, spread her gossamer wings, and flew off.

A heavy day was it with Giant Selfishness; his mind was full of anxiety and fear. What if the chosen knight should resist the temptation—if, resolute in the way pointed out by Conscience, he should neither indulge in the dainties so treacherously provided, nor follow the light sent to mislead! As the night closed in and the scene grew darker and darker, with huge strides the giant sought his pit in the wood; there, like a wild beast lurking in his den, he awaited the approach of Fides—he dared not stand the stroke of the invincible sword, but he might slay his foe if taken at disadvantage.

Ah, how many times, whilst indulging in the feast of Gluttony, had Fides heard the faint warning voice of Conscience! But, proud of his success in his conflict with Sloth, he regarded not warning nor danger. The sound of the clock fell unheeded on his ear, and not till the darkening shades told of the approach of night, till the glass ceased to sparkle, and all grew dim, did he slowly rise to depart.

Giant Selfishness crouched by his pit in the woods, and listened for the sound of footsteps. For a long space he heard only the rustling of the leaves, as the night wind moaned through the forest. The stars scarcely gleamed in the dark blue sky, through openings in the driving clouds. At length a light appeared at a distance, and by its yellow, flickering beams the giant knew it to be the torch of Pleasure. On it came, nearer and more near; and now the flash of its gleam upon armour, and the sound of a footstep on the forest path, showed that a knight was fast following behind. Then Giant Selfishness rubbed his huge hands with delight. "He who follows only Pleasure," he muttered, "will be sure to fall into my pit."

The Giant Crouched at the Pit

The sword of Fides hung by his side—it was not in his hand, for he found it encumber him as he passed through the thicket. He was not on the watch for a foe; he thought of nothing but the gay light before him.

Suspecting no danger, he pressed on with rapid step; then, ha! there was the sound of a crash and a cry; he had reached the pit, he had set his foot on the edge, he had fallen into the snare of Selfishness.

The fall did not kill him, though the pit was deep—perhaps his wondrous armour protected him from severe injury—but he was bruised, mortified, and discouraged; and the giant whose art had thrown him into this dark prison was resolved to keep him in it till he should perish by a slow, lingering death, as thousands had done before him.

But Fides, the conqueror of Sloth, was not one to remain a captive to Selfishness without making an effort to escape. He was not content to be shut out from usefulness and glory; he had fallen, indeed, through his careless walk, but he might yet struggle up to freedom. As soon as the knight fully understood his position, he began to attempt to climb the sides

Fides Follows Pleasure

of the pit, for the armour which had been given to him never encumbered his motions—though strong in the battle, it yet sat light on the wearer as a garment of silk.

A few small twigs of the creeping plant which in that land is called "Desire of Approbation," gave some little hold for his fingers, as he tried the difficult ascent. With great effort he reached about one-third of the height; then the spray which he grasped broke off in his hand, and he fell again heavily to the bottom, while the laugh of the giant, from the brink of the pit, mocked his disappointment and pain.

Fides was not, however, altogether discouraged; he resolved to take a better and surer way. His own strength would not suffice, but then he had his sword; he would cut out resting-places for his feet in the soft wall of the pit, and thus find a method to rise. He cut them, with a strong and patient hand, as far as his arm could reach, with many a thought of his King. He placed his foot on the first, raised his other to the second, and then, difficult as the task had become, and sorely as his arm ached with the exertion, scooped out two more little notches above his head. It was dark, and the giant, who, kneeling by the edge, with his head bent down, was glaring into the pit, could not see his intended victim; but he heard the sound of the earth as it fell, and caught a glimpse of the point of the sword, working its difficult way.

"Ha! that must be put a stop to!" cried Selfishness, as, hastily gathering together a heap of stones, earth, and turf, he hurled it down in the direction of the climber. The mass fell first on the sword—the invincible sword, which the weight of a mountain would not have snapped. This broke the force of the blow; but it was still sufficient to dash the weapon from the hand of Fides, and hurl the knight once more to the bottom.

Now was Fides in sore dismay, and much he repented having lingered so long at the feast, and forgotten Conscience to follow Pleasure. He felt almost tempted to despair of ever getting out of the pit of Selfishness. He felt in the dark for his sword; he found it, and tried its edge—it was keen and perfect as ever. Then remembering the words of Conscience, in his distress he breathed upon the hilt. In a moment a faint light shone in his prison from the star-wreath round the brow of his friend.

"O Conscience!" exclaimed the unhappy prisoner, "never before hast thou seen me in such woeful case! Must I remain buried alive in this pit—am I shut out from the kingdom forever?"

"Thou must climb," replied Conscience; "though thou hast fallen thrice, he who perseveres must be successful at length."

"But my limbs are bruised and weary, my strength is half-spent. When I rise a little way, down comes a shower of earth, which throws me back into my dungeon. I have nothing firm upon which to lay hold; nothing to help me to rise from these depths."

"Look this way," said Conscience; "see what has been placed here to enable poor captives to climb up from their dungeon." By the soft light which she threw around her, Fides perceived a cord of twisted silk and gold hanging from the top of the pit.

"This," continued the guide, "is the strong cord of Love: the bright scarlet twist is love towards man; the golden— stronger, holier love. The giant knows of this cord, and a thousand times has tried to break, or loosen, or destroy it; but it is not in his power to do so. Sometimes, indeed, he draws it up, so that his victims cannot reach it; either he has forgotten this precaution to-night, or he has trusted that the darkness would hide from thee the means of safety and deliverance."

Fides grasped the slender but firm cord of Love, and with stronger hope, and more steady resolution,

In the Pit

41

again began his dangerous ascent. The climbing appears far easier now; his feet find the notches prepared in the wall, and relieve his arms of a portion of the weight. But Selfishness, meanwhile, is not idle above; again he collects a heap of stones and of earth, but in the deep darkness, uncertain of his aim, while the mass comes crashing and thundering down, but a small portion actually strikes the knight. Another upward step, his hand is on the edge of the pit; one more, and his head rises above it. Then Giant Selfishness utters a cry of despair; he has no courage to cope with the invincible sword; he turns his back like a coward upon his foe, and is slain in the act of flight.

Fides stood panting and breathless, scarcely believing his own victory—exhausted with his efforts, but rejoicing greatly in their success. With his drawn sword in his hand he stood, when a faint cry for mercy struck on his ear; and, caught in the thicket by her gossamer wings, her bright torch lying extinguished on the ground, by the dim twilight which was now appearing he recognized his false guide, Pleasure.

Doubtful he stood, with his weapon raised, unwilling to strike a creature so fair, unwilling to destroy what possessed such power to charm, yet resolved to do his duty, whatever it might cost him.

"O Conscience!" he cried, "come now to my aid. Must Pleasure be destroyed when sin is overcome?"

The starry one was again beside him. "Hold thy hand," she exclaimed, "and let Pleasure live, now that her master, Giant Selfishness, is slain. She shall be thy servant, even as she was his; but she must first learn how to perform higher, nobler tasks than any to which she was accustomed with him. I will place her beneath the care of Benevolence, where all her better nature will be drawn out; Pleasure will then

The Death of Selfishness

become a holy thing, her office no longer to lead thee astray, but to follow thy footsteps in the path of duty, and remain thy companion for ever!"

"Ah, I am glad that poor Pleasure was not killed!" exclaimed Laura

"A dull life she would have of it with Benevolence," observed Constantine.

"I don't think so," said Aleck, glancing up from his drawing;" and I am certain, at least, that it would be a much longer one than if she had remained the servant of Selfishness."

"How do you make that out?" exclaimed several voices.

"Why, Pleasure is fairly worn out by Selfishness," replied Aleck, who was naturally a reflecting boy. "He kills her by working her too hard. The greedy boy eats for pleasure, suffers for it afterwards, and pleasure is destroyed. The selfish boy thinks of nothing but his own amusement—no one cares for him, no one loves him—and pleasure is destroyed. The—"

"The moral is this," interrupted Mrs. Roby, who saw that her son was treading upon dangerous ground: "Our business is not too eagerly to follow pleasure, but if we do our duty pleasure will follow us. What mere selfish enjoyment can compare with the delight of feeling that we have cheered the sad and helped the distressed, that we have poured sweetness into a bitter cup, or led one poor wanderer into the right way! This is a pleasure that will never die; it is pleasure like that which is enjoyed in heaven!"

CHAPTER 5

GIANT UNTRUTH

Hesaid Laura to her sister, as they sauntered in the garden alone. "Did you not like to hear all his grand stories about his home?"

"No," was Bertha's brief reply. "What, not about driving in a carriage with four horses, and being trusted with the reins himself, and being introduced to the Prince of Wales, and having a game at leap-frog with him!"

"I did not believe a word of it, nor, I am sure, did mamma," replied Bertha; "did you not see how very grave she was looking?"

"I never thought of that," said the innocent little child; "I never supposed that Pro was so wicked as not to speak the truth."

"He thought it a good joke to take you in," replied her sister.

"I will never believe anything that he says again. Yet Pro

is pleasanter than Con, after all."

Pro and Con, it may be here mentioned, were the familiar names given to the Probyns by Aleck, and adopted by his sisters.

"Well, I'm glad that you think so, Missy," said Adolphus, who had overheard her last words, as he strolled into the gar-

In the Garden

den with his ball in his hand, throwing it up and catching it again as he slowly sauntered along. Adolphus was not an ill-natured boy, and was rather inclined to make friends with the little rosy cheeked damsel beside him, so he challenged her to a game at ball. Bertha, who wished to water her flowers, left them alone together.

"Now, Missy, could you hit that nail on the wall?"

"I'll try," cried the child, eagerly, flinging the ball.

"You're not within a mile of it!" said Adolphus.

"A mile! Oh!" exclaimed Laura, who had never been accustomed to the evil habit of exaggeration.

"Now, look at me, I'll knock it flat—no—I see that I've aimed a little too high; run and fetch the ball, like a good child."

"Pro, I think that you had better not throw that way any more," said Laura, as she ran panting back with the ball.

"And why not, pussy?"

"Because you might fling it again over the wall, you know—you throw so much further than I can—and the glass cucumber-frame is just at the other side."

"Oh, there's no fear, little Prudence; I shall take care. I'll hit the nail to a dead certainty this time there!" as he spoke the ball whirled through the air, and disappeared over the wall.

"A miss; but I'll do it next time!" cried Adolphus. "Off for the ball, I'll try it again."

Once more the willing little messenger started, but she returned with a slower step, and a very grave face as she said, "The cucumber-frame is all smashed—I picked the ball out of the middle of it."

"Dear me—that's a pity; but it can't be helped now. You won't peach, that's a good girl."

"What's that?" asked the innocent Laura. "You won't tell of me?"

"Not unless I am asked."

"And if you are asked, you can easily say that you never saw any one breaking the glass frame.

"Oh!" exclaimed Laura, opening her eyes very wide, with an expression of indignant honesty.

"Why, you stupid little thing, you would be saying nothing but the truth; how could you see any one breaking the glass frame with that great brick wall hiding it from us completely."

"But I am sure that you broke it."

"That doesn't matter a pin. I don't want you to say that you do not *know* who broke it, but that you did not *see* it broken by any one."

"There's no difference," said Laura, looking puzzled.

"There's a great deal of difference," replied Adolphus, impatiently; "the one would be an untruth, the other"—

"An equivocation," said a quiet voice behind him.

Adolphus started on seeing Mrs. Roby.

"My dear boy," she continued, laying her hand upon his shoulder, "do not attempt to silence conscience by the idea that by such a pitiful evasion you could escape the guilt of untruth. A falsehood is an attempt to deceive; there may be falsehood where words are strictly true, there may falsehood where not a word is spoken."

"I don't see how that can be," said Adolphus.

"There is falsehood in suppressing the truth, as well as in saying what is not true. If a man whose pockets are full of money puts on an appearance of misery, and receives charity which he does not require, that man is acting a falsehood. If a boy silently accepts praise for a generous action which he knows that he has not performed, or has performed from some unworthy motive, his very silence is a kind of falsehood."

"I don't think that we can help telling untruths in this world," said Adolphus. "Why, there's my aunt, who is so terribly particular, I know that she does not like her neighbour Mrs. Rogers at all, and yet, when she was obliged to write a note to her, she called her 'My dear Mrs. Rogers,' and signed herself Yours sincerely.' I am certain that Mrs. Rogers was not dear, and that aunt could not be sincere when she wrote that."

"Do you think that Mrs. Rogers was deceived by the letter, that it made her believe herself a favourite with your aunt?"

"Oh no; there was nothing in it to make her think that—it was all about recommending a nurse."

"Then there was no sin of untruth in the letter. The beginning and ending were mere forms, placed as a matter of course, like a wafer or a seal; they were not intended to mislead, and they did not. Had your aunt warmly grasped the hand of the person whom she did not respect, embraced her, made her understand by her manner and her smiles that she valued and loved her very much, there would have been deceit and hypocrisy then, though not a word of untruth might have been said."

It was probably the above conversation that induced Mrs. Roby to choose for the subject of her next chapter,—

Fides now prepared to depart from the scene of his fall, and also the scene of his victory. Leaving Pleasure in the hands of Conscience, he only asked his bright friend what new achievement demanded his efforts now.

"Giant Untruth must at once be attacked," she replied. "He is one of the most dangerous of thy foes, from the strange enchantments which he uses. One stroke will not lay him low; he bears a charmed life, and thrice must he feel thy sword ere it has power to destroy him. A giant though he be, he can shrink to a shape as small as that of the tiniest dwarf, and so remain concealed and unnoticed till his pursuer passes by, and then, resuming his own form, strike at his foe unawares."

"A hard task is before me," said Fides, "How shall I find out an enemy who hides himself thus—how discover him in his secret haunts?"

"Hold up thy glittering sword on passing any suspected place. If no Untruth lurks there, no change will be seen; but if the shadow of the blade falls near the false one, a dark shade will appear on the object that conceals him: strike then, strike boldly, and Untruth will fall!"

A few more words of counsel from his friend, and the champion departed on his way.

Seen from a distance the Castle of Untruth appeared like a lordly palace, on near approach it showed like a poor-house. What had seemed marble was now seen to be but painted lath; the stately turrets were nothing but a deceptive wall; the large mullioned windows were false ones, admitting no air and no light; the very bolts on the door only seemed to be iron—they gave way to the first stroke of the sword.

But if the outside of the Castle of Untruth was so mean, far more so was the dwelling within. No beam of day ever struggled into that place, bats hung from the rafters above, damp trickled down the green unwholesome walls, the trail of the serpent was upon the floor, and the yellow glare of sickly torches rather dazzled the eyes than guided the foot-steps of the stranger. Where is there upon earth a lower, baser spot than that where Untruth has fixed his abode!

Fides proceeded along a narrow crooked gallery called Fear, which occupied a great part of the dwelling; through this gallery the giant received countless victims, who, lost in its dreary mazes, groped their way into the presence of the destroyer. Perhaps Conscience, unseen, guided her champion now, for he neither stumbled over the obstacles that lay in his narrow path, nor struck his helmet against the low roof which seemed ready to fall in, nor missed his way in the labyrinth of Fear.

Just as the gallery ended in a large dimly-lighted room, Fides caught a glimpse of the giant before him. Never had he seen anything so hateful to the eye, so repulsive to the generous soul. None of his race was more hideous than Giant

Untruth; meanness, cowardice, and cunning were stamped upon his brow; he looked like one who would shrink from the light. For a moment Fides beheld the giant, then, as if by magic, Untruth vanished from his eyes, and the knight found himself, as it appeared, alone, to pursue his search after his artful foe.

There were many strange objects in that hall, not one of which, when closely examined, looked the same as it did

The Giant Untruth

when at a distance. Treasures of plate, golden vases, candelabra of the same precious metal, proved to be nothing but gilded tin; imitation jewels gave a mock splendour to the place, and the tables were heaped with glittering coins which were only made to deceive. Fides, however, amidst so much that engaged his attention, was resolved not to forget his first important object, to hunt out Untruth wherever he might lie hidden. At one end of the hall the knight's eye was struck by a very large and handsome mask that rested against the wall. The features wore a smiling expression, the complexion was of a beautiful white; Fides fancied—was it only a fancy? —that through the eye-holes of the huge mask he saw something moving behind!

Straightway he approached it with his wondrous sword; even as its shadow fell on the false face a dull stain appeared on the whiteness of its brow. Down came the blow, so heavy and so sure, that the mask in a moment was cleft in twain, and Untruth, receiving his first wound, rushed forth from his hiding-place and vanished.

This success made Fides more eager in pursuit; with rapid step he moved from place to place, examining this, glancing under that, keeping sharp watch, like a good champion as he was. Now a heap of dresses thrown loosely together in a corner excited the suspicion of the knight. Amongst them was one cloak* of white fur, lined with black, whose massive folds might conceal the enemy. The test of the sword was applied to this; darkness gathered on the whiteness of the fur, its hue grew like that of the lining within, —again down came the stroke, again the traitor felt its power, and fled to hide for the last time from the invincible sword.

Fides pursued his search till he was weary, and inclined to rest content with the success which he already had gained.

He had examined every spot, as he believed, again and again, had paced through the length and the breadth of the hall; was it not possible that Untruth was already slain? He wished to believe this, and yet felt a doubt on his mind, which prevented him from resting at ease. He sprang up from a heap of cushions on which he had been reclining, determined to pause no more in his search till the enemy should be found. Thrice he passed along the hall, thrice examined the gallery of Fear, then returned to the hall disappointed, but not altogether discouraged.

The Mirror

Amongst the curious furniture of the place was a mirror which possessed the property of magnifying every object before it. It was set so close to the wall that there appeared to be room for nothing behind it, and thus it aroused no suspicion in Fides. Viewed in this mirror, a dwarf would swell to a giant, the smallest thing appeared large, the meanest became great—it at once magnified and distorted. Fides stood still for a moment to look at his image in it, and smiled at his own stately height, and the size of the arm which he raised.

"What a mighty sword will mine appear magnified thus!" he exclaimed, as he turned the clear blade towards the mirror. But scarcely had its reflection appeared upon the glass, when Fides started to behold the gathering stain which dimmed all the lustre of the crystal. Collecting all his strength for a final blow, Fides dashed his good sword against the surface, shivered the false mirror into a thousand pieces, and slew the Enchanter, who, in his narrow recess behind, had been laughing at the vain attempts to discover him. Such was the end of Untruth.

CHAPTER 6

TRIALS AND TROUBLES

Dear mother, you look very pale, " said Bertha, as soon as the tale was concluded.

"I am not feeling very well, my love; I have one of my headaches to-day. Perhaps I may be better after dinner."

"We must make no noise for mamma," whispered Laura to Adolphus, as they were summoned by the bell to the meal.

Mrs. Roby carved—that was always her office; in every little duty of the kind she spared her husband all trouble that she could possibly take on herself. But when she had supplied the children's plates, Bertha remarked that she put nothing on her own; she rested her head upon her hand, and closed her eyes, as if she were in pain.

"Mamma eats nothing," whispered Laura again, a look of anxiety on her bright little face.

"My love, are you not well?" said Mr. Roby, laying down his own knife and fork.

"I do not feel as well as usual," she replied, with a faint smile, her face growing paler, her eyes heavier, each minute; "I believe that perhaps I had better go to my own room, I am not good company for you to-day. "She rose, but almost staggered as she rose, and was glad of the support of her husband's arm. Her children followed, anxious and unhappy; their mother was ever so cheerful and bright, so thoughtful of others and neglectful of herself, that they feared that she must feel very poorly indeed to leave them thus, and retire to her bed.

"Oh, go back to your dinner, my children," she said, with a half-vexed, half-gratified look, as she saw the three at the door of her room. "This is nothing to make you uneasy; I only require a little rest and sleep. I hope that I shall soon be all right again. Go, return to your young guests below." Laura only stayed for one kiss, and then went away with her brother. Bertha lingered to beat up the pillows, bring out the cloak, draw the window-curtains to keep out the light, and then, taking the hand of Mr. Roby, left her mother to try to get a little sleep.

Feeling unhappy about her suffering parent, and disinclined to touch another morsel of her food, Bertha was irritated to see Adolphus eagerly helping himself from the dish, having taken possession of her mother's vacant chair.

Little was said during the remainder of the meal, after which Bertha, creeping with noiseless step up-stairs, returned with the good tidings that, on gently opening the door, she had seen her mother fast asleep.

"On no account disturb her," said Mr. Roby, rising." I am obliged to go to see a sick parishioner; I depend upon the house being kept quiet in my absence."

"But, papa, it is raining so fast!" said Laura.

"Poor Thompson is dying," was her father's reply; "if I delay, I may never see him alive. I think your dear mother said that she had a little broth ready; I will carry it to him myself."

The Probyns were diverted to see the dignified-looking master walk off in the rain, struggling to hold up an umbrella against the wind so as to protect both himself and the brown jug in his hand, and picking his steps through a river of mud.

"He'll spill it, to a dead certainty," laughed Constantine.

"I'd drink it on the way, just to put it out of danger!" cried his brother. Their loud rude voices sounded in strange contrast to the low tones of the Robys, whose minds were full of the illness of their mother.

"Oh, Aleck," whispered Bertha, going close up to her brother, and laying her hand on his arm, " what on earth can we do to keep these Probyns quiet? Unfeeling boys that they are, what a noise they are making! They will waken poor mamma; they will make her head worse. Oh, what are we to do to keep them both still?"

"I say, Pro, would you not like to take a book?" asked Aleck.

"You know I hate books—I am going to drive four inhand," replied the boy, dragging the chairs towards the black horse-hair sofa, which he proposed to convert into a coach.

"I'd have a railway-train," cried Constantine; and, raising his hands to his lips, he gave a loud whistle, in imitation of the sound so familiar to travellers.

"Oh, be quiet!" exclaimed Laura; "you forget mamma!"

Constantine's reply was a whistle twice as loud.

Aleck was about to say something in a high, angry tone, but was stopped by poor Bertha's imploring look.

"Can't we make them think of anything else?" she whispered hurriedly to her brother; "we might employ them in making a kite."

"A good thought," replied Aleck; "but where are we to get the materials?"

"You know that you have the laths and the large sheets of paper ready, and as for string, there is plenty in that drawer, and"—

"Shall we set to, and make a famous kite?" proposed Aleck aloud to his companions.

To the relief of Bertha, the idea pleased both the Probyns; for once in their lives they appeared quite agreed.

"We must have lots of paste, to begin with," said Con.

"Run to Susan, Lautie dear, and ask her to make a little," cried Aleck. Sweet little Laura was ever the ready messenger, and had darted off before the sentence was concluded.

"What a comfort Aleck is; I don't know what we should do without him!" thought Bertha, as she saw him setting about the kite-making with energy and skill, making even Adolphus busy. "Now I can slip quietly away, and sit at dear mamma's door, and

Bertha at Her Mother's Books

58

watch till she wakes, and get her tea the first moment she wants it."

So there the loving child took her station, listening for the slightest sound from within, distressed when any loud voice or laugh from below broke the quiet stillness of the house.

"I am afraid that I am selfish, sitting here doing nothing," Bertha said at length to herself. "Dear mamma is always so active and busy, on Saturday evening above all. There is so much mending to do—ah, could I not help her in that? But I do so dislike mending and darning; it is the most tiresome work in the world!" The little girl heaved a sigh. "I fear that I am in the pit of the giant, but I must struggle out of it as well as I can; my work-box is in the sitting-room, how vexatious! I did not wish to go there again. Perhaps, after all, the mending may be left alone for just this one week." She paused irresolute, and sighed again. Then words came into her mind which had been taught to her by her beloved mother, holy words about being "not slothful in business;" it was plain to Bertha that Conscience was rousing her to work, and, with a resolution worthy of Fides himself, she ran down-stairs for the work-box.

"We must have scissors—scissors!" were the first words with which she was received.

"Give us your scissors, Bertie; quick!" cried Con in a domineering tone.

Now Bertha disliked the request for more than one reason. She did not like the manner in which it was made; she did not choose to part with what she might require herself; and she was afraid to trust rather a delicate pair of scissors in the hands of rough, "fiddle faddling boys."

"Laura, where are yours? They are commoner, they are

less likely to be spoiled," said she.

"Oh, I can't find them—Giant Sloth has hid them somewhere!" laughed the child.

Bertha thought the laugh unfeeling when their mother was unwell, and felt provoked at the carelessness of her sister.

"Come, quick, I can't wait—out with your scissors!" repeated Con.

Bertha gave them, but with no very good grace, and with an irritated spirit returned to her station at her mother's door. Oh, this pit of selfishness! how hard it is to climb out of it, step by step!

Bertha now began to think again of her plan for assisting her mother in mending, but recollected that all the clothes collected for that purpose were in Mrs. Roby's own room, which could not be entered without risk of awakening the invalid. Bertha felt more glad than a perfectly unselfish girl would have been, at being thus prevented from attempting a tiresome task, especially as there was a very amusing book which she wished to finish before Sunday.

Bertha was soon deeply engaged in her book, when she was interrupted by little Laura running up-stairs, and saying softly, "Bertie, the boys want your paintbox."

"But they can't have it," replied Bertha, with impatience; "they would make such a mess of all my nice paints, and spoil the whole box, that I have been keeping so carefully that I have scarcely liked to use it myself."

"They want it very much; I shall only have to run up-stairs again," said Laura, as she slowly and reluctantly descended the stairs with the ungracious message of her sister.

The next minute a door below was noisily opened, and Con shouted out in a loud, angry voice, "Bertha, we must have your paint-box!"

"Oh dear, he'll wake mamma!" cried Bertha, in distress; "Yes, yes, I'll bring it directly, only be quiet," she whispered, leaning over the banister.

"Bertha!" called a faint voice from within the room.

The little girl entered it with a noiseless step. "Is anything the matter, my love?"

"Oh no, dearest mamma; only that boy Con wanted something. I am afraid that he awoke you with his loud voice. Do, do go to sleep again; it will do you good."

Mrs. Roby's eyes closed heavily.

"Do you feel better, dearest mamma?"

"I hope to be better to-morrow," said the lady, faintly.

"May I sit beside you, my own precious mother?" whispered Bertha, her heart growing very heavy.

"No, no; go and do what the boys want, my love; I need nothing but rest and quiet."

Bertha kissed her mother's feverish brow, and glided out of the room, but not without the bundle of clothes which had been placed on a chair ready to be mended. With a sigh she drew from her drawer her beautiful little paint-box. She opened it, and taking out the two cakes which she most admired, the light blue and the lake, put them carefully by amongst her little treasures.

"I will save these, at least," she said to herself; then fearing lest delay should occasion another loud call from the impatient Constantine, she ran hastily down with the box.

The sitting-room presented such a scene of disorder as might have been expected, and seemed a copy, in a small way, of the hall of Giant Sloth, in everything but its stillness. The table was covered with lath and paper, cuttings of which strewed the carpet; books and boxes were huddled together on the chairs; and a tangled heap of twine lay on the floor, which Laura was trying to draw out into some order. Con, with his sleeves tucked up and his hands all over paste, of which some had found its way to his jacket, snatched the paint-box eagerly from Bertha, upsetting, as he did so, the glass of water which had been placed ready for the painting. "Why were you so long?" he cried, angrily.

"Your loud voice awoke mamma," said Bertha, reproachfully; Aleck and Laura uttered exclamations of regret.

"Well, I'm sorry for that, but it was your own fault. Why,

Bertha's Paints

how's this," added the boy as he opened the box; "here are two of the best paints gone! Have you hid them to keep them from us?" he cried, turning fiercely towards the frightened little girl.

Bertha's heart beat quick; she thought of Giant Untruth, and the gallery of Fear; but whatever other faults might be hers, she was never guilty of this most disgraceful one. She did not give an equivocating answer; she did not say, "Perhaps they may be up-stairs," or, "I will go and try to find them;" to the question of Constantine she returned a simple truthful " Yes," and never had the boy respected her so much before.

"Well, that's candid, at any rate," he said, with a smile; "but I should not have thought of your being up to hiding them."

"She had a good right to do what she pleased with them," observed Aleck; "and it is kind in her to lend us any of her paints. Here, dear," he continued, addressing his sister, laying his hand on the box, which Con had placed on the table, "we shall only want these, the yellow and the red; take the box with the rest of them up-stairs, they might get spoiled here amongst us, you know."

There was a glow of grateful affection towards her brother in the heart of poor little Bertha as she heard this proposal, to which, to her surprise, the Probyns made no objection. Perhaps there was some good in them, after all; perhaps they thought, from seeing the example of Aleck, that it is quite as manly to be considerate and courteous to a little girl, as to bully, tease, and distress her; that nothing is gained by fretting the tempers and embittering the lives of those with whom wed well, while the affection of a young warm heart is not a thing to be thrown lightly away. It is doubtful whether these thoughts entered the minds of Adolphus and Constantine—if they did so, it was probably for the first time; but it is certain that Bertha left the room with a feeling of tender, grateful love towards Aleck. He was making her duty less difficult to her, he was helping her out of the pit of Selfishness, he was holding out to her grasp the strong cord of Love—she would have given up anything to please him.

"How strange it is," such were the reflections of Bertha, as she commenced her self-imposed task of mending—"how strange it is that I should think so much of doing a trifle for her to whom I owe everything! I have heard that when I was very ill, as a baby, mamma never went to rest, night after night, but carried me about, rocking me in her arms, till she was scarcely able to stand. How good she has been, teaching me all these long years, slow, troublesome pupil as I have been! How often have I wearied her, and tried her patience; looked vexed when she reproved me, and not heeded her advice! Oh, if I were to lose her now!" The tears rose into Bertha's eyes, and her work seemed to swim before her. "If I could only be a comfort to her, save her trouble, never give her another moment of pain, repay—oh no! I can never repay, but show how I feel all her tender love. Now that she is ill"—here two great drops fell on the sock which Bertha was darning, and there was the sound of a little short sob, but she stifled it lest her mother should hear it.

Just then Bertha heard voices in the hall. Mr. Roby had returned, and with him a medical man whom he had met at the cottage of Thompson.

"I should like you to see her. I trust that her indisposition is slight, but—

Bertha rose with her finger on her lips, but a little noise in the room within showed that precaution was not needed. The doctor saw Mrs. Roby, and pronounced that her illness was not of an alarming nature; that it had been produced by over-exertion, and that, therefore, quiet and repose were indispensable for the present. For at least this and the following day, the lady was not to quit her own room.

Great was the relief of her loving family on hearing the opinion of the medical man; a weight seemed taken from the heart of poor Bertha, but still care and anxiety pressed on her mind, greatly increased by the thought which was perpetually recurring,—"When mamma is not here to look after us, how shall we ever manage with the Probyns?"

CHAPTER 7

SUNDAY AT DOVE'S NEST

O h, let me love this blessed day, the best of all the seven!"—

Were the words which came into Bertha's mind as she opened her eyes on the Sabbath morning. "Ah, I am afraid that I shall not do so to-day!" was her next feeling. "When mamma was with us, singing hymns and reading the Bible to us, and telling us all about holy things, then, indeed, Sunday was a happy day; but now I expect nothing but difficulties. I am sure that the Probyns will not care to do as we have done, and they will not be kept to lessons with papa as they are on week-days; mamma took our Sunday teaching herself. Oh, what shall we do without her!" and, for the first time in her life on a Sunday morning, Bertha wished that the evening had come.

Yet the sun shone out so brightly, the rain-drops which

hung from the fresh green leaves danced so gaily in his beams, and the flowers gave out such a delicious scent, that it seemed wrong to be dull and anxious when all Nature was rejoicing around. Then Bertha had the comfort of hearing that her mother had passed a tolerable night, that her head was greatly relieved, and her fever almost subdued. Laura's face looked like sunshine itself, Aleck's manner was even kinder than usual, the breakfast went pleasantly over, and nothing occurred to give a feeling of discomfort till, Mr. Roby having retired to his study, his children and the Probyns were left in the sitting-room together.

"We had better go on as if mamma were with us," said Bertha softly to her brother, unclasping her little pocket-Bible. "We can repeat our texts to each other."

Aleck looked doubtfully at the Probyns, who were carelessly turning over some books which lay on the table. "We shall hardly get them to do anything," said he." I wonder if they have ever learned the Catechism?"

"They won't repeat it to us, if they have. We must just do what is right, and leave them alone."

"I will go to my own room," said Aleck, rising and taking his Bible with him.

"Laura, come and I will show you what verse you should learn, and hear your Catechism up-stairs," said Bertha, as soon as her brother had departed.

Laura was looking over the pictures in the "Children's Paper" with Adolphus, and seemed rather unwilling to move.

"You'd rather stay with us, wouldn't you, Lautie?" said he, playfully pinching her rosy cheek.

"Laura, when dear mamma is not well, we ought to act just as if her eye were on us," cried Bertha, with some emotion in her tone.

Laura's Detention

"She does not want your preaching; she is not your slave!" cried Constantine in an insolent, provoking manner, which brought the colour up to the very temples of Bertha.

"Perhaps I ought to go,"whispered Laura, trying to disengage her little hand from that of Adolphus; but he only held it the tighter.

"Laura, you know how naughty it is"—began Bertha, but Constantine again cut her short,—

"If you mean to set yourself up as mistress here, you will find yourself pretty much mistaken. You'll please to march off double quick," and, suiting his action to his words, he pushed her rudely out of the room.

Bertha ran up-stairs, almost choking with passion hot tears overflowing her eyes, burning feelings of anger in her heart; she was ashamed in her excited state to appear before either her mother or Aleck, so, rushing into her own little room, she flung herself down on her bed, and buried her face in her hands. "Oh, I do hate them—I can't help hating them! I wish—oh, how I wish that they had never come here! I was wanting so much to do what was right, to be a comfort to mamma, and to take care of Laura. What a trial this is! I never shall bear it. I'd rather live on bread and water than go on in this way!"

She sat up on her bed, and as she did so caught a sight of her own face reflected in a glass. She dashed away her tears directly.

"Aleck must not see me; he would think that mamma was worse. Oh, what an ungrateful girl I am," she cried suddenly, "when my precious mother is so much better, to let anything fret me thus! If she had been very ill— dangerously ill— oh, that would have been a trial indeed! I must do what papa tells us so often to do—think of my blessings rather than of my vexations. He says that in every trial which is sent us faith will discover some good;—I wonder what good there can be in this; what good can come from these Probyns being here!"

Again Bertha rested her head on the pillow, but she was now a great deal more calm. She thought of her mother's words, "They are teaching you to know yourself;" and she felt that the last few days had certainly given her insight into her own heart, such as she had never possessed before. "Perhaps, also, I needed patience to be more exercised," thought she; "I require a great deal of it now. But it is hard to have such a constant struggle—no peace, no quiet, no comfort. Ah! Perhaps this is what mamma means to teach us in the story of the champion Fides. He was not allowed to rest and be idle: when he had conquered one enemy, he had instantly to prepare for some brave attack upon another. Perhaps life may be a fight all the way through. I never thought of that before."

Bertha's reflections were broken in upon by a little soft

hand that was gently laid upon hers.

"I came as soon as I could—indeed I did," said Laura; "but they were so full of play. Oh, you have been crying, Bertie!" she added, as she saw her sister's face; "dear, dear Bertie—I am so sorry—I'll come directly next time!" The little arms were pressed close around Bertha's neck, and the curly head rested on her bosom.

A quiet, peaceful half-hour was spent together by the sisters. Bertha seemed quite to have recovered her usual tone of mind. A short time was then passed with their mother; after which the whole family, with the exception of the invalid, proceeded to the church of which Mr. Roby was the minister.

"Here, at least, there will be peace," thought Bertha, as she entered the walls of the ivy-mantled building, and heard the sweet tones of the hymn. But, alas! Even in the house of prayer unworthy, unholy thoughts will too often intrude. Bertha, accustomed to perfect reverence and quiet behaviour in church, was annoyed beyond measure at the conduct of the

The Sisters

Probyns. Constantine was fidgeting, staring about him, turning round on his seat; Adolphus yawned loudly and repeatedly during the sermon, though preached by her own venerated father. The angry emotion which took possession of

The Children at Churcch

Bertha's mind quite destroyed all peaceful enjoyment of the service; while Aleck, though apparently following the prayers very devoutly, as he was accustomed to do, was scarcely conscious of the act in which he was engaged, but was passing secret comments in his own mind on the shocking behaviour of his companions. He was wondering at the neglect of the parents who had brought them up, thinking how he would act towards them were he in the place of his father, devising plans of very rigid discipline, which, as it seemed to him, ought to be adopted; and, in short, was unconsciously quite as inattentive a listener to the prayers as those whom he so strongly condemned.

This was no longer the case, however, as soon as the sermon commenced. With his eye fixed upon his father, and his ear drinking in every word which he uttered, Aleck forgot even the presence of the Probyns.

"You must know the sermon by heart, for you neither

winked nor moved a finger from beginning to end, while I was almost asleep!" laughed Adolphus, as the children proceeded home together from church.

"I always write out as much as I can remember of the sermon between the two services," replied Aleck, who was secretly a little proud of his talent in this way. "I write it out, and so does Bertha."

"Oh, I do but little!" said his sister, who was ever on her guard against untruth, even in his least startling disguise; "sometimes I only put down the text."

"I shall do less," observed Adolphus, "for I shan't put down anything at all."

"You spoke of two services," said Constantine; "you don't mean to say that you go to church twice?"

"Laura does not—she is too little; but we who are older are allowed to do so," replied Aleck, with a little testiness in his manner.

"Oh, but we don't want to be allowed!" laughed Constantine; "I should say that we've had enough for one day."

"We'll stay at home with little Laura," cried Adolphus.

Aleck gave a meaning glance at Bertha; they both felt hurt at the indifference shown to the preaching of their beloved father, and they easily mistook this sentiment for one of indignation at the Probyns' carelessness on the subject of religion.

After dinner Aleck went to his room to write down the sermon, as usual; while Laura and Bertha enjoyed a quiet, happy time with their mother, who, greatly recovered, was now able to sit up a little in her arm-chair. Then, when the soft, musical church-bells summoned again to the house of prayer, Aleck and Bertha proceeded with their father along the green pathway, overshadowed with elm-trees, which led to the little church.

Bertha was happier during this service than she had been in the morning; but still, though the Probyns were not present to distract her mind from holier things, she often found her thoughts wandering to the subject which so painfully engaged her now.

"Aleck," said she to her brother, as they walked quietly home together, Mr. Roby having remained behind to have some conversation with the schoolmaster—"Aleck, do you not find it hard not to dislike the Probyns?"

"I don't dislike—I despise them," was Aleck's reply.

Bertha said no more, but walked on, wondering to herself whether it were as wrong to despise as to dislike; and whether those who were as good and clever as Aleck might not look down on the ignorant and ill-behaved.

Her reflections were disturbed by an exclamation from her brother, as he swung back their green door, and caught sight of the lawn. There were Pro and Con, in riotous mirth, rushing along, as far as the narrow space would permit, with the painted kite floating in air above them, and little Laura racing at their heels, joining her merry voice to theirs.

"Sunday—a clergyman's lawn — a pretty sight for all the village!" cried Aleck, running hastily forward. His indignation was greatly increased by his well-founded suspicion that the tail of the kite, which had been left unfinished the night before for want of paper, had been supplied from the pages of one of his own well-written copies.

"You forget where you are—you forget what day it is!" he exclaimed, laying his hand angrily on the string to draw down the kite.

"Take that for your meddling!" cried Constantine, turning fiercely round and striking young Roby in the face. The blow was instantly returned, and the next moment the two boys were engaged in fight.

Aleck knew nothing of boxing, and had never had a battle before; his blows were ill-aimed, and, though taller than his opponent, he very soon felt himself over matched. Adolphus stood by cheering on his brother, and laughing at the misery of poor Laura and Bertha, who, at the unaccustomed, and to them most terrible sight, ran about in an agony of distress, imploring the boys to desist, and calling out for some one to part them. Aleck was on the ground; he struggled up again, his face all streaming with blood; Bertha, almost wild at the sight, rushed forward and clung to the arm of Constantine, again raised to strike at her brother.

"Unfair! Unfair!" gasped Constantine.

The Fight

"Unfair! Two to one!" echoed Adolphus.

"Shame on you, boys!" cried a manly voice, which the children recognized as Mr. Roby's. With two ladies at his side, he now stood by the lawn; and the sound of a window hastily opened above, showed that his wife also, alarmed at the sounds from below, was a spectator of the painful scene.

In a moment the two combatants fell back, and stood panting, flushed and excited, with their hands still clenched and their lips compressed, but their eyes turned towards Mr. Roby.

"What is all this about?" said the clergyman, sternly. He had to repeat the question before a reply was given; but then a torrent of answers burst forth at once from all the children— each eager to tell his own story.

"He hit me."

"He insulted me"

"He was tearing down our kite"—

"Oh, papa, only see how Aleck has been treated!"

"Send them away—send those cruel, cruel boys away!" Laura and Bertha could scarcely speak through their tears.

"I will examine into this; both parties shall be heard. Constantine and Adolphus, retire at once into my study. Aleck, you had better go into your own room, and let Susan see to your hurts. I am grieved that this should have happened at any time, but, above all, that it should have occurred on a day when you have all met together in the house of prayer."

Aleck, holding his handkerchief to his face, and followed by his sisters, ran into the house, and was met on the stairs by Mrs. Roby, looking very pale, indeed, but more composed than her daughters. She drew him into the room which she had just quitted.

"Laura, ask Susan to bring some hot water; Bertha, my

love, you must not agitate yourself thus. I trust that we shall see that little injury is done; he will soon be all right again."

"I am so vexed, mother, at anything occurring to annoy or fatigue you when you are not well," exclaimed Aleck, as Mrs. Roby, with her cold, trembling fingers, gently bathed his face with warm water.

"Oh, look at his poor eye!" exclaimed the terrified Laura; "will it ever get like the other again?"

"Does it hurt you very much, dearest Aleck?" cried Bertha.

"Oh, I don't care for the pain," muttered Aleck, "if only he had not had the best of it; but to be beaten by such a boy! well the time may come"—the rest of the sentence could not be heard, but his mother guessed its meaning very well.

"A time may come," she said, in her own gentle tones, "when my Aleck may be victor in a far nobler fight."

"O mamma," cried Bertha, "surely he acted nobly! He only fought that wicked boy because he was doing what was wrong."

"If we fight every one who does wrong," replied Mrs. Roby, with a faint smile, "we must have to give battle to the whole world; and as we must begin with ourselves, I think that we had better proceed no further till we are conquerors there. Now, my boy, I hear your father calling you downstairs; as your hurts have been attended to, you can go to him at once. I trust that this will be the last time that any of his children will cause him this pain and alarm."

Aleck departed, and Laura stood crying at the end of the couch, upon which her mother had reclined herself again. "Mamma, I was so naughty," she sobbed; "I would not go with them at first—but somehow—I forgot"—

"You forgot your parents' wishes and your own duty, my

Laura. But you are so unhappy already—you have suffered so much—that I will say no more on the subject. Go and look over your pretty 'Children's Paper,' my love; and if you could learn a little verse from my favourite hymn, it would be nice employment for Sunday evening."

Mrs. Roby's voice was growing faint. Laura bent over to kiss her mother, and left a warm tear on her cheek. Bertha remained in the room, silent and thoughtful, wondering what was going on in the study, and what punishment her father would inflict on the offender. "I hope that he will be flogged!" At length she exclaimed, unconsciously uttering her thoughts aloud.

"I do not think so," said Mrs. Roby; "I believe that your father intends to pass over the first offence. Besides, your brother may have given provocation."

"The first offence!" exclaimed Bertha, her face full of anxiety almost amounting to terror; "why, mamma, Con won't be allowed to stop here to fight anymore—he will be sent away to-morrow morning, I'm sure that he will; won't he be sent away, mamma?" she continued, in an earnest, imploring tone.

"I do not think so," was again Mrs. Roby's reply.

"Oh, but this is dreadful—dreadful!" cried Bertha, clasping her hands; "he will owe Aleck such a grudge, and they sleep in the same room, and they will be always fighting, with no one to interfere, for Pro is just as bad as his brother. Oh, mamma, if you had only seen him standing by and laughing, and shouting out, 'Give it to him,' and 'Hit him in the eye'"—Bertha's words were interrupted by her tears.

"We shall find some means, my love, of stopping all this; fighting shall not be permitted in this house. It ill becomes any Christian home; above all, the dwelling of a minister of the gospel of peace."

Bertha had sunk down her head upon her hands; she now raised it, tears streaming from her eyes.

"Mamma, I shall be afraid even to say my prayers as long as these Probyns are allowed to stay here."

"To say your prayers!" repeated Mrs. Roby in some surprise.

"You have told me that I dare not ask to be forgiven if I do not forgive, and I cannot—I cannot forgive Constantine Probyn!"

"Bertha, can a Christian child utter such a word!"

"I know that it is wrong, but I cannot help it. I struggled to keep down my angry spirit as long as he was only unkind to me; but to see my own darling brother treated in that way—it is more than anyone could bear."

"My child, the stronger this feeling is in your heart, the more need you have of the assistance of prayer. Have you asked for a spirit of forgiveness?"

Bertha hung down her head in silence.

"Have you asked that a better heart may be given to those whose faults cause so much pain?"

"Pray for the Probyns! Oh, I should never have thought of doing that! I despair of their ever changing."

"That despair arises from want of faith. Their faults have been nurtured by indulgence; the soil, I grant you, is overrun with weeds, but that is no reason why we should give up its culture in despair. We must soften the hard ground by kindness, we must pray for a blessing on our labours, we must work on in patience, forgiveness, and love, and who knows how great our reward may be at last!"

"Do you really believe it possible that these Probyns can ever become like Aleck?"

"Quite possible, my dear, and not unlikely, I trust. We shall have something to bear from them at first—we must look for no sudden change; but even if they were never to improve, if they were to remain our daily trial for years, should not we, in performing our duty towards them, find a sweet satisfaction in the thought that we had not suffered our own passions to master us, that we had fought a good fight with the secret foe within?"

CHAPTER 8

GIANT HATE

Mrs. Roby had judged truly of the intentions of her husband. Bertha never knew exactly what had passed during his long interview with her brother and the Probyns, but she soon found both that Constantine would escape punishment this time, and also that he was not likely to repeat the offence. There was no more fighting between the boys, but there was a bitter, uncomfortable feeling, which perhaps was an evil as great, because more difficult to be entirely overcome.

Mrs. Roby resumed her place in the family circle almost before her health made it prudent for her to do so. Her presence seemed ever to work like a charm; before her smile the fierce glance of Constantine grew mild, and Adolphus appeared almost agreeable. She seemed, like the summer sun, to draw out all that was good from the most unpromising soil. Her character could not fail to inspire respect, while her unvarying kindness won affection. Hers was seldom the open rebuke before witnesses, to arouse the spirit of pride and rebellion; but the quiet word of advice, the gentle warning in moments when the heart was softened; and what she said, though sometimes little heeded when spoken, came back on the hearer's mind. She did not take open notice of the too evident dislike between her children and her guests, though she inwardly grieved to see how much of an unholy nature remained in those whom she had hitherto brought up in peace and love; but she had patience—oh, how much patience is needed by a mother and while she neglected nothing that might be a remedy for the evil, she cast her cares upon a higher Power, and trusted that she would be helped in her labour of love.

Affairs were in this position at Dove's Nest when, a few days after the occurrences related in the last chapter, Mrs. Roby produced her continuation of the story of the Giant-killer.

Giant Hate

Deep in the recesses of a wood, not far from the Castle of Untruth, a warm, bubbling fountain gushed from the earth. Even in the coldest winter, when icicles hung from the boughs of the overshadowing trees, that spring rose hot and steaming to the light. Some said that a subterraneous fire must have given this strange property to the water, some that Giant Hate, the owner of the ground round it, had mingled in it some secret venom. Thus much was known to all, that no moss or green herb would grow where the spray fell from the warm spring of Anger, and that whoever drank of its waters became at first furious, then helpless and feeble, an easy prey to the giant of the place.

One bright day when the sunbeams bathed the world in light, and the little birds sought the shelter of the thickest foliage, stilling their songs till the soft evening breeze should arise to cool the fierce summer heat, Fides, passing through the depths of the woods heated and thirsty, arrived at the fount. He had been passing through a difficult and tangled way, torn by the thorns that stretched across his path, annoyed by the insect tribes that haunted the wood, and provoked by the insolence of the inhabitants of the land, who, being themselves the subjects of Giant Hate, annoyed his foe from a distance with poisoned darts, called "bitter words," which gave a most painful, though not dangerous wound. The lips of Fides were parched and dry, his shield hung heavy upon his arm, and the sound of water as he approached the spring made him quicken his footsteps to reach it.

Certainly a sweet, cool stream would have looked more tempting to the weary traveller than the heated fount, with the light steam curling above it; but, warm as it appeared, it was not too hot to drink, and Fides eagerly scooped up the water with his hand.

"Beware!" cried a soft voice in his ear. The knight well knew the tones of Conscience; he paused for an instant she knelt by the spring, but whether his thirst was too great to bear delay, or whether the fumes rising from the tainted fountain of Anger disturbed his judgment and weakened his power of self-control, putting his head down to the level of its basin, he drank greedily of the intoxicating waters.

Their fatal effect was seen only too soon; Fides started up from his knees in wild frenzy—he attempted to draw his invincible sword, but that could never be unsheathed but in a good cause, and remained fast fixed in its scabbard. Passionately he slung it from him—he tore off the armour which he wore, piece by piece, in the madness which now possessed him—struck at every object that happened to be near—injured himself in his furious rage - reason, conscience, all seemed lost in a moment to the victor over Selfishness, Sloth, and Untruth. It was a sad, a grievous sight to behold in the once faithful champion the victim of Hate; either when the poison boiled in his veins, flushed his cheek, and kindled a wildfire in his eye; or when, exhausted by his own passion, the knight sank to earth, helpless, defenceless, with scarcely power to move.

Then darting from the ambush in which he had lain concealed, Giant Hate rushed upon his foe. In the state to which his own folly had reduced him, Fides was unable to make any resistance. He was bound tightly, cruelly bound with cords by the giant, till he could scarcely stir hand or foot. Now did it appear to Fides, as his reason gradually returned, that he was in worse case than when struggling in the pit of Selfishness. He knew that he was reserved for a cruel death—for these giants were never known to show mercy—and when his enemy left him in solitude for a while, bitter complaints burst forth from his lips.

"Oh, wherefore did I drink of the fountain of Anger,—must I perish the captive of Hate! I, who overcame Selfishness and trampled on Untruth!—I, to whom so glorious a reward was offered—to whom so faithful a guide was given! Must I now lose all, disgrace the name that I bear, and furnish a cause of triumph to the enemies of my King! Oh, Conscience! Conscience! Would that I had listened to thee, that I had never tasted of that fatal spring!"

Conscience, ever near, appeared visible before him; but how was her aspect changed! The stars on her brow wore a red, angry hue, the kindly expression of her face was altered

The Giant Hate Capture

to one stern and terrible.

"I warned thee," she cried, "but thou wouldst not hear! Thou art overcome—disgraced—endangered!"

"Oh, chide me no more!" exclaimed the suffering knight; "help me in my weakness, assist me in my peril, let me not die in the hands of my foe."

"What can I do for thee," sadly replied his guide; "I have no power to cut the cords that bind thee; Conscience alone cannot release from Hate. The invincible sword can be wielded but by him to whom it has been given at the first and lo! Thou hast cast it far from thee."

"Bring it back to me, Conscience!" implored the fainting knight; "let me at least die with my hand on the hilt."

The bright one obeyed: Fides touched again the invincible sword, but his weakened hand had no power to unsheath it. A little way, indeed, he drew it from its scabbard, but not enough to render it of any avail in severing the tight cords that bound him.

"I am doomed, I am doomed!" he bitterly exclaimed; "no strength is left in my feeble arm, the poisoned waters have done their work." Fides turned his face to the ground, and uttered a deep groan of despair.

"Hope still," cried Conscience; "thou mayst yet be freed. See, rising far above all the trees near it, yonder fair, stately palm. The name of that tree is Forgiveness, the fruit that it bears are called Benefits; both they and the juice which distills from the stem are a powerful cure for the poisons of Hate, and destroy the effects of Anger. Who knows but that thy strength may be restored to thee yet, that thou mayst live on for freedom and victory!"

So saying, raising from the ground the bright helmet which Fides had cast away in his madness, Conscience hastened to the healing tree, and while Fides with effort and pain still struggled to free himself from his bonds, she drew a cooling beverage from the stem.

A wondrous tree was that of Forgiveness; the deeper the wound inflicted on its trunk, the richer and freer its waters gushed forth, so sweet and pure, that it was a marvel that any thirsty pilgrim who knew the refreshment that they yielded could turn for a moment aside to drink at the fountain of Anger.

Fides partook of the healing draught, and a change seemed to pass over his whole frame. He no longer felt the excitement of fever, or the painful weakness which succeeds it—his fingers no longer helplessly grasped the sword which he could not draw—as well as his bonds would let him, he gradually unsheathed its blade—once more it glittered in his hand; and though the giant's cords made it difficult to wield, each effort which Fides made rendered the next more easy. He cut the bonds one by one, and stood erect, ready once more to fight the battles of his King.

The knight replaced his sword in its sheath, gathered up the armour so madly thrown away, and thanking Conscience at once for her warning and her aid, prepared to seek out Giant Hate and destroy him.

While fastening his helmet on his head, Fides noticed a quiver full of sharp, poisoned darts, which the giant had dropped on the ground when he had bound the knight by the fountain of Anger.

"These are 'bitter words,' exclaimed Fides, "the weapons of the giant and his followers, those which he so often discharges at his foes. I have felt their sharpness before now, and have been tortured by the venom which they bear. Now they are in my hand, and I can use them. I can launch them with an unerring aim at the enemies against whom I am not permitted to draw my sword. But let me reflect," he continued, still grasping the poisoned darts; "are these weapons which it is lawful for me to use? are they such as become the champion of my King? Are not 'bitter words' strictly forbidden to all to whom the invincible sword has been entrusted? Never will I stain my holy cause by instruments so unworthy!" he exclaimed, as he snapped the venomed darts one by one, and flung their broken fragments into the dust. Even as he did so, a soft, pure radiance fell around him for an instant; it was not the glow of the noonday sun, it was not the glance of the summer lightning—he knew it for the smile of approving Conscience.

Hardly had the gleam passed away, leaving a sweet remembrance behind, when Fides was half-tempted to regret that he had thrown from him the sharp weapons of Hate. The people of the neighbourhood, long beneath the giant's sway, had gathered together to mock his opponent, bound and helpless as they expected to find him. On they came with "bitter words," contemptuous looks, and scornful jests; and though they paused on perceiving that Fides was now free, collecting together they prepared to surround him, and annoy the brave knight from a distance.

Fides laid his hand on his sword, but it was not to be moved from its scabbard; it was given to be wielded in fight against the giants of sin, not turned against his own fel-

The Rabble

low-creatures. Fides felt for a moment helpless and irresolute, not fearing death, but insult and pain, with the fiery darts which he now might have used lying all broken at his feet.

A moment's reflection, however, restored hope to the breast of the knight; where healing had been given, refuge might be found; with a bound he burst through the circle of his tormentors, and began to climb the tall tree of Forgiveness. Rapidly Fides ascended the stem, while his enemies gathered round the foot of the tree.

They beheld him now seated among the branches at the top, looking down upon them from the lofty height of Forgiveness.

"Our darts can reach him yet," cried the foremost of the troop; and while a rude burst of laughter sounded from below, a shower of stones and darts was flung high in air, more than one of which struck, and even wounded the knight.

Well then was it for Fides that he had chosen as his refuge a tree possessing powers of healing. Rich, ripe clusters of Benefits were growing before him; he hastily plucked one, and from the stalk whence it had been torn oozed out the precious balm. With one hand Fides applied the healing drops to his hurt, with the other he flung down upon his enemies below Benefit after Benefit, as fast as he could throw them. Quickly the shower of fruit descended on the heads of the persecuting band; this was his return to the stones and the sharp venomed darts with which they had annoyed him.

As Fides bent from the branches to mark the success of his new mode of warfare, he saw the crowd eagerly gather up the ripe fruit, and, with a wondering glance at the source whence it came, drop their darts to commence their delicious repast.

Even as the waters of Anger produced a strange effect upon those who drank of them, so Benefits, the fruit of the tree of Forgiveness, seemed to work a change upon those who partook of them. Insolent looks grew mild, angry voices gentle, the storm of passion became hushed and still. The savages themselves broke their darts, and gazed up with strangely altered feelings upon the champion of order and peace.

At length one who had been foremost of the band, most rude in his insults, most bitter in his words, advanced with a frank kindly air, and thus addressed the knight in the tree:

"O Fides! we own ourselves overcome; thou hast returned evil with good, and wrongs with Benefits, thou hast weapons which none can resist. Think not that we now shall be thy foes, or that we willingly bear the yoke of the giant. He is a tyrant, tormenting and destroying: there is no sweetness in the waters of Anger, no joy in the service of Hate! Comedown, then, and attack our enemy and thine; if we aid not in the fight, we will rejoice in the triumph. Since we have eaten of that tree, all appears in a new light to our once blinded eyes; we have learned to distinguish our foe from our friend, and we look for our freedom from thee!"

With a thankful spirit, and hopeful of victory, Fides now commenced his descent. Scarcely had his foot touched the ground, when an exclamation from one of his new allies gave him warning of the approach of the giant. Fides firmly grasped the hilt of his sword, and now, with scarcely an effort of his arm, the good blade flashed in the sunlight, as if eager to strike to the dust that barbarous enemy of man. The crowd, gathering in a circle, gazed as spectators on the terrible fight. Hate, arrayed in a blood-red mantle, with a heavy mace in his hand, seemed likely with every blow of his deadly weapon to crush the light form of Fides. But the champion had a source of strength which failed him not in the hour of danger. His helmet was not broken by the strokes which fell so heavily upon it, his armour gave not way in the fight, and his courage remained firm and unshaken. At length, seizing a moment of advantage, he plunged his sword into the heart of Hate, and, with one cry of dying rage, the giant expired at his feet.

Then were there great rejoicings amongst those who of late had suffered from his tyranny. The people willingly dug a wide grave in which their tormentor should lie buried forever. Willingly, at the command of Fides, they brought heavy masses of stone to choke up the fount of Anger. A short time

The Conflict

after, no one who passed by the place would have recognized the once gloomy spot. Where the heated waters had dried up the verdure, now the soft moss spread its carpet of velvet; and the fragrant violet and the lily of the valley shed their blossoms over the grave of Giant Hate!

"This is the strangest story that we have heard yet," cried Constantine; "pelting with Benefits, what a curious idea!"

"I should think the vanquished better off than the victor," observed Adolphus, "feasting upon that famous fruit."

"Oh no!" exclaimed Aleck; "Fides looked down upon them all," and he glanced rather contemptuously at the Probyns.

"You're not Fides, nor anything like him!" retorted Constantine; and as Aleck felt the warm fount of Anger bubbling up in his own heart, he could not deny the truth of the assertion.

"Oh, Fides did wrong at first," cried Laura; "but then he listened to Conscience, and snapped the poisoned darts, and climbed up the tree of Forgiveness. I don't see why we should not conquer like that brave knight, after all."

"Conquer our enemies—conquer ourselves," thought Aleck, and it struck him how much nobler that conquest would be than any of the triumphs of genius. He glanced at his sister Bertha, and it seemed from her look as though the same idea were crossing her mind; while Constantine was reflecting (for he sometimes did reflect) that his own position had hitherto been that of one of the mocking crowd; that the power of giving annoyance is one which we share with the insect and the reptile; and that there is something degrading in being the slaves of our passions, or the subjects of Giant Hate.

CHAPTER 9

FAIR GRATITUDE

From that day the children of the Roby family firmly and prayerfully resolved to struggle against the
enemy within, and, if possible, by benefits overcome
those whom they regarded as the enemy without. Instead
of exciting each other to anger by complaints of annoyance
from the Probyns, they agreed to unite all their powers to
render their difficult duty more easy. If gloom gathered on
Bertha's brow at some unreasonable request from Adolphus,
the smile of Aleck reminded her of the victory over the giant;
if her brother flushed at an insolent word from Constantine,
he caught the quiet glance of Bertha's eye, and was silent.

Where the darts of "bitter words" are broken and thrown
aside, passion usually dies away. Aleck and Bertha both en-
deavoured to keep a bridle on their lips, and their efforts
were not all in vain. Constantine, who had some generosity
in his nature, grew ashamed of offering provocation where
none was returned, and Mrs. Roby, with a delight which few

but a parent can fully understand, watched the growing improvement in her children. Their patience, their forbearance, were increasing under trial; their virtues were becoming strengthened by practice; they knew more of the difficulties of the Christian fight, but they also knew more of the spirit which overcomes them.

The Probyns also were not exactly the same as when they had first been received into Dove's Nest. It is true that we do not uproot in a few weeks the weeds that have been suffered to spread for years—that habits of order, obedience, and self-denial are usually of slow growth, because not natural to the human heart; yet some improvement might be seen, though small, to encourage hope for the future. Adolphus and Constantine had been not as those who fall into the pit of Selfishness, but as those who are born and brought up in its depths. The pleasure of thinking of others, living for others, giving up their own will for the happiness of others, had been as unknown to these boys as the brightness of the sky and the beauties of Nature would be to one who had always dwelt underground. They now began to have an idea that we are born for something more than merely to eat and drink and amuse ourselves; and, with the example of the Robys before him, Constantine felt sometimes half-inclined to lay hold, like Fides, on the twigs of "love of approbation," and win praise by showing a little kindness. His motives, however, were too weak, his selfishness too strong, for him yet to make much progress, and his pride was ever in his way.

Adolphus, on his part, was certainly more upon his guard against the enemy Untruth. He had little need to search for him behind the mask, for hypocrisy was not in his disposition; but equivocation, usually the result of fear, had become, alas! but too familiar to the boy; while, until he became the pupil of Mr. Roby, Adolphus had scarcely ever related an occurrence without falling into the error of exaggeration.

"There are hundreds of sheep in that meadow!" he exclaimed one day.

"Hundreds! It scarcely appears so to me," was Mr. Roby's quiet reply; "will you oblige me by counting the exact number?"

Adolphus, a little annoyed, had to comply; there were not more than forty in the field.

"Then, taking your statement at the lowest, your hundreds but at two hundred," said the clergyman, "by how much has the glass of exaggeration multiplied the number of the sheep?"

"Oh, I'm not half so slow as you think me!" cried Adolphus at another time, when some observation had been made about learning; "I can get twenty stanzas by heart before breakfast!"

"Have you ever tried to do so?" inquired Mr. Roby.

"Oh, I've done it fifty times!" cried the boy.

"If you have done it fifty times, you will easily do it fifty-one," said Mr. Roby; "I shall expect you to bring the stanzas to-morrow morning:" and he rose from his seat to take down a volume of poetry from the bookcase.

The countenance of Adolphus fell; he was ashamed of his silly boasting, and afraid of the consequences which it might bring upon him. He had no alternative but that of either confessing that he had spoken nonsense, or studying hard till noon before breakfast could be touched; so, mortifying as it was, he chose the former course, and was far more guarded in his speech in future.

Several interruptions had occurred to postpone the reading of " the Giant-killer," but one noon, the little party being

Exaggeration

assembled around her, Mrs. Roby continued as follows:

Fair Gratitude

The life of Fides was not one of rest: he well knew that fresh labours were before him, but his was a joyous, gladsome heart; he felt honoured by the permission to serve his King, and to devote his strength to the cause that he loved.

One autumn evening, when the red orb of the sun was setting behind a bank of clouds, tipping their edges with golden light, as Fides was passing along the side of the morass of Forgetfulness, he thought that he heard a faint cry. He paused to listen, for by a champion of the Truth the voice of distress is never heard in vain. Wide and dreary the swamp lay before him; not a tree broke the dismal expanse, but rank weeds grew thick in many parts, with rushes that seemed bending beneath the white mist that spread like a pall over the morass. Their presence betokened that of water; but no silvery sheet reflected the fading splendour of the setting sun, the mantling green upon the pools shut out the light, and filled the air with unwholesome odours. Remembrance of the past may be painful, when we review our mistakes and recollect our errors; but better, far better, to wander even over the painful desert of Regret, than to lose sense of both pleasure and sorrow together in the fatal morass of Forgetfulness. Again that cry, even more faint than before; but Fides felt certain that he heard one. As his sight could scarcely pierce the gathering mist, he lifted up his voice and shouted. From the swamp an answer was returned, as from the voice of a woman in distress.

"Help! help!" it cried, "for I am sinking! In the slough of Forgetfulness I shall be lost."

Fides hesitated for a moment, then his resolution was taken; whatever might betide him in the attempt, he must venture to the rescue of the sinking sufferer. With a light and springing step he bounded forward some little distance in safety, and could now see, not far from where he stood, the form of a woman struggling in the swamp. But between her and him lay a part of the morass too soft to be traversed securely, though the ground upon which the knight rested his foot was firm. Then a thought came to the mind of Fides, and he instantly acted upon it. The long cord of twisted silk and gold, by which he had climbed from the pit of Selfishness, he had borne along with him ever since, wound in many a fold round his form. He speedily unrolled it, and grasping one end, he fastened his shield to the other, and then flung the buckler, with a strong arm and a steady aim, in the direction of the sinking woman.

Fides Saving Fair Gratitude

She touched it, grasped it, laid hold upon it, as one who, when drowning, clings for life; and by means of the soft, bright cord of Love, Fides gradually drew her to firmer ground, where the trembling one might rest in safety.

As she thanked him fervently again and again, the earnestness of her manner giving force to her words, her voice tremulous with emotion as she spake, Fides thought that a being more exquisitely lovely his eyes had never beheld. The angel sweetness of her face told of a spirit pure, loving, and holy; every movement was full of grace, and it was no marvel that the world, enchanted with her beauty, had surnamed her Gratitude the Fair.

"Gentlemaiden!" said Fides, "by what strange misadventure hast thou fallen into yon dangerous swamp?"

"I was flying from my enemy, from stern Giant Pride, from him who seeks to destroy me. The very name of Gratitude is hateful to his spirit, he would slay me if he could; or if not, drive me forth to dwell among savages or the beasts of the field. Even with bears—with lions I would be safer far than with him! He tracked me this evening as, hard by this place, I bore home a large basketful of Benefits, which I had been gathering in order to preserve. The instant that Pride saw me, he pursued me: I dropped my burden in the haste of my flight; and though I fled yonder where he dared not follow, I beheld him with insolent scorn scatter my fruit over the waters of the morass. I fear to meet him now on my homeward way—I shall perish by his cruelty at last."

"Fear not, Fair Gratitude," replied Fides; "this sword shall be drawn in thy defence; sooner will I die than suffer thee to be destroyed, thou that art beloved of all the children of virtue. Let me escort thee now to thy home; then, without delay, will I seek out that giant who would sink Gratitude in Forgetfulness."

So Gratitude led Fides towards her dwelling, and much they discoursed by the way of the giant who was now to be overcome.

"Pride is a prince amongst the giants," said the maiden; "not one has greater power than he. He is also one of the most artful of thy foes; he can often assume the manner and garb of a citizen of thy land, and he can speak its language in a way to deceive even an experienced ear."

"How then shall I know him?" asked Fides.

"He speaks the language well," replied the maiden, "but yet is unacquainted with the character in which it is written. This, Pride has never learnt, and by this thou mayst easily detect him. But there is a friend of mine, named Experience, who dwells not very far from this place; when thou hast passed over the hill to our right, the sound of his hammer on the anvil will be thy sure guide to his forge. From him thou mayst gain knowledge more than I can give— he will direct thee to the haunts of the giant. He will also tell thee of a marvellous and precious thing, which once belonged to the treasury of thy King, but was stolen thence by the giant. A high and glorious reward has been offered to him who will restore to its rightful owner the golden staff of the Will. Mayst thou have strength to wrest it from Pride!"

"And may I be granted strength to free thee from thy persecutor!"

"Thou hast already slain one foe to me and mine," replied Fair Gratitude. "I was long an object of the hate of Giant Selfishness, since I helped to fix by his fatal pit that cord of Love with which thou hast since saved me. Once was I myself almost stifled in the pit, but Experience came to my succour."

"I have often heard of thy name, Fair Gratitude," said Fides, "but I never beheld thee before."

"I have been much talked of in the world, but little known," she replied. "Thousands have eagerly promised to make me their companion till death, but on their way to my home have turned back, or been lost in the morass of Forgetfulness."

By this time the maiden and the knight had reached the dwelling of Gratitude. A small, humble abode it appeared, with a doorway so low that Fides had to stoop his plumed helmet ere he could enter. But no sooner was he within the place, than he gazed with admiration around. He found himself in a goodly dwelling, lighted by a beautiful silver lamp, which cast soft radiance like moonlight; and in diamond letters glittered the word "Memory," inlaid in the clear metal. It was the daily occupation of Fair Gratitude to keep this lamp perfectly bright; with her own hand she fed it with precious oils, which shed a delicious perfume through the place.

By the mild light of Memory, Fides beheld that the room in which he stood was hung round with exquisite pictures, all of which represented scenes beautiful to the eye and pleasing to the heart. In one a mother was tenderly bending over the cradle of a helpless babe; in another, a father, with the best of books open before him, was instructing a fair-haired child. One picture showed a poor widow receiving aid from a generous friend; the next, a truant led back by an elder companion to the path which he had lost, half struggling, half resisting, and yet clinging to the guide, whose looks told of pity and love. An open door led into an inner apartment, even fairer and more preciously adorned than the first, into which Fair Gratitude often retired for the purpose of prayer and praise; for this was her dearest occupation, this was her highest delight.

After Fides had passed a short space of time in examining the pictures hung round the walls, and had received from Gratitude minute directions as to the way to the dwelling of Experience, who could guide him to the haunts of Giant Pride, he took his leave of the gentle maiden. She stood at the doorway to see him depart on his dangerous but glorious mission; and there, as she lingered, with the faint moonbeams gleaming on her lovely form, her clasped hands, and her soft flowing hair, Fides thought that she looked like an angel of light blessing him before the battle. Still as he pursued his onward way, he could fancy that he beheld Fair Gratitude yet, trimming and feeding her silver lamp, and gazing fondly on the pictures that reminded her so sweetly of the past.

Fair Gratitude Watches Fides Depart

Laura had edged her little chair nearer and nearer to her mother as the description of the dwelling of Gratitude was read, and her curly head was resting on the knee of her parent at the close. The Probyns sat silent, thinking, perhaps, what pictures Gratitude should hang up for them. They had been accustomed to receive kindnesses with pleasure, indeed, but without any idea of keeping a thankful remembrance of those to whom they were indebted for them. Pleasures, when once over, had to them left nothing behind; they had not lighted the silver lamp of Memory in their hearts to renew joys and bring the past back again. They had not yet, like Aleck and Bertha, known the deep, sweet feeling of Gratitude, which, beginning with duteous love towards the parents who have watched over our childhood, extends to every friend whose kindness has cheered us, and rises most noble, most holy in its nature, towards the Giver of all that is good.

Where Pride and Selfishness hold their sway, alas! too often it is found that Gratitude—a virtue despised or unknown—is lost in the swamp of Forgetfulness!

CHAPTER 10

THE PLEASURE EXCURSION

On the succeeding day, which was the anniversary of the birth of Mrs. Roby, the children were permitted to make a picnic excursion to a thicket on Upland Hill, and as it lay at some distance from Dove's Nest, a conveyance was hired to carry the party thither.

A small pony chaise was accordingly brought to the door, and into it the young people cheerfully hastened, provided with a basket of sandwiches, cakes, and biscuits, and the best fruit which Mr. Roby's garden could supply.

It had been usual for Mrs. Roby to accompany her children in their annual expedition to Upland Wood, but her place in the small vehicle was now more than filled up by the addition of the two young Probyns, and she could not therefore join the party without depriving someone else of the treat. With many a word of advice and kind injunction, she

Starting on the Picnic

suffered the children to depart without her. Aleck, who was exceedingly steady, and had been taught enough of driving to be trusted with the reins of such a very quiet pony as Dobbin, sat in front, with Constantine beside him, while the larger back seat was fully occupied by Adolphus, the two little girls, and the basket of provisions.

Off they drove, a merry little band, and all went on well as heart could wish as long as they remained within sight of Dove's Nest; but then Constantine, in his proud, domineering manner, insisted on driving the pony himself. "There is no fun," he cried, "in sitting idle in the carriage;" and he attempted to seize the reins from the hand of Aleck.

Aleck at first resisted, words became high—he had been intrusted with the charge of driving-—he would not give up his post to another—for aught that he knew, Constantine had never touched a rein before.

"That's little that you know," angrily retorted young Probyn; "I've driven my father's two spanking grays, rather different from this wretched little pony!"

Aleck had never known Constantine guilty of an untruth, and therefore, though surprised, did not doubt his assertion. The fact was, that both Constantine and his brother had more than once been allowed to hold the reins, while the powdered coachman sat beside them on the box, watchful to prevent any mischief from ensuing from the indulgence granted to his young masters. Aleck now, sorely against his will, relinquished what was to him a great pleasure, to prevent the pleasure of the expedition from being marred by anything like a quarrel at the outset.

His little act of self-denial seemed, however, at first to have small effect in preserving peace, for no sooner had Constantine gained the driver's seat, than Adolphus, who was as ambitious of the place as his brother, and even more selfish in his disposition, began to urge his claims, and struggle to enforce them.

"Let Con drive to the wood," said Aleck, turning round where he sat, and laying a firm hand upon the shoulder of Adolphus, who was in the act of clambering over from the back seat; "I will take care that you have the reins on your return, if you wish them;" and, only half satisfied with this assurance, young Probyn fell back into his former place.

But the incapacity of Constantine as driver was pretty soon evident to all the party. Aleck, seeing his ignorance, offered a few hints, but the proud boy disdained to take advice, and only further betrayed his want of skill. Dobbin, indeed, was the most quiet of ponies, and had his rein been a silken thread, held in the little hand of Laura, he might have proceeded very soberly in his own way, and landed them all safely at last. But Dobbin did not understand being beaten, and having his mouth pulled hard at the same time; he did not know whether he was intended to go forward or to go back, and probably not wishing along drive with such a charioteer, he very obstinately decided upon the latter. Instead of proceeding to Upland Wood, he half turned the carriage round, and, amid the sound of Constantine's blows, Bertha's entreaties, Aleck's advice, and exclamations of alarm from little Laura, Dobbin fairly won the victory, for he backed the chaise into a ditch and overturned it!

A spectator might have been disposed to laugh at the scene, as, except a strain of the left shoulder which Constantine received, and a few slight bruises to the other boys, none of the party were injured at all.

They all scrambled out of the ditch as well as they could, Aleck and Adolphus laughing and joking on the funny ap-

The Spill

pearance which they presented, but Constantine rising from the mud in a little pain and a very great passion. Bertha quieted the fears of her little sister, smoothed her own crushed bonnet, and turned with a smile to the boys, who were endeavouring to drag the carriage out of the ditch, while Dobbin, a little heated with his exertions, stood very patiently by.

"Oh, but I say, this is no joking matter!" exclaimed Adolphus, stopping in the middle of a jest, when he saw the basket of provisions half-covered with mud in the ditch—all the preparations for the picnic quite destroyed. Every one looked grave at the sight, until the piteous expression of little Laura's face tickled the fancy of Aleck, and made him laugh in spite of the misfortune.

"I vote that we go back for more," said Adolphus.

"No!" exclaimed Constantine, in an angry and determined tone, for he had no wish to meet his tutor or Mrs. Roby at that moment; he felt that he had been playing a ridiculous part, and he could not bear to be laughed at.

"We'll do very well till dinner-time," said Aleck; "there are plenty of blackberries in Upland Wood; we'll picnic upon them and contentment."

By this time the boys had succeeded in dragging the little chaise out of the ditch, but so bedaubed and be splattered with mud, that Bertha and Laura felt hardly inclined to get into it.

"We'd better walk home, perhaps," half whispered the latter to her sister.

"Nonsense! Get in, will you!" growled Constantine." Pro, leave that basket alone; there's nothing there fit to be eaten, even by a glutton like you."

"Glutton!" exclaimed Adolphus, angrily; "no one likes to see his dinner in a ditch. I think that it would have been better for you to have said nothing about the matter, as it was you who brought us into this pickle!"

"It was that brute of a pony!" cried Constantine, savagely; "if I won't give it to him! Where's the whip!"

"In my hand," said Aleck, calmly but firmly, "where it shall remain for the present."

Constantine looked ready to spring at him; but there was a quiet determination in him who held the whip, which showed that Aleck would now be as resolute in keeping his proper place as he had before been good natured in yielding it.

"Con, you shan't drive any more," cried Adolphus; "we've had enough of ditches for one day." The looks of the girls expressed much the same as Probyn's words.

"I wouldn't drive such a mule!" said Constantine, contemptuously; "Aleck is heartily welcome to make what he can of it; we shall never arrive at the wood."

Aleck jumped up in front, Adolphus beside him—the latter never offering to drive, as, after what had occurred, he stood rather in awe of the pony. Constantine looked as if he were doubtful whether he would enter the chaise at all; and it would have been well for the pleasure of the party had he decided on not doing so, for he came in with the manners and in the temper of a bear, squeezed Bertha up into a corner, half crushed Laura's little foot, and never opened his mouth but to say something provoking.

"We shall have to fight with Giant Hate all the morning," thought poor Bertha; "the tree of Forgiveness is very hard to climb—almost more so than the pit of Selfishness. How I wish that there were some way quite to choke up the fount of Anger in our hearts, so that it should never come bubbling up again!"

The little girl was in the position of one fighting and struggling against an enemy almost too strong for her; but she had broken the venomed darts; to the many "bitter words" of Constantine, she returned not one.

It by no means improved the temper of the boy to see how quietly Dobbin trotted on with his new driver; he scarcely needed a touch of the whip, and, in spite of what Constantine had foretold, they did arrive safely at the wood. This was a great relief to Bertha, for here the children separated at once. The Probyns went off in different directions to search for blackberries, which were abundant; Aleck, after tying up Dobbin, for whom Laura delighted to gather long handfuls of grass, mounted the hill to enjoy the fine view from the top; and Bertha, now feeling like a bird set free, began to look round for wild flowers.

"Laura, pet, you must help me to gather some," she said, "to make a beautiful crown, as we did last year, to give to dearest mamma on her birthday."

"Oh yes," cried Laura, eagerly; and first giving Dobbin's rough coat a friendly pat, she ran off to assist her sister.

"Look what beauties I have found!" said Bertha; "we have no such wild flowers near us. Is it not fortunate that my own little basket was not crushed when the chaise was

Making the Flower-Wreath

upset. I brought it on purpose for the flowers."

"Ah, the poor basket in the ditch!" laughed Laura. "I almost think that it would have been better for us if the empty basket had been crushed, and the full basket saved. Pro would think so, I am sure of that!"

A happy time it was for the little girls, as they pursued their pleasant occupation, consulting together whether red, white, or blue flowers should have the principal place in the crown, and which was the prettiest, and imagining how pleased their dear mother would be when their present was placed before her. Their enjoyment was increased when Aleck returned to them, bringing blackberries which he had gathered for his sisters; he also plucked for them some wild roses which were beyond their reach, to add to their floral treasures. He had scarcely left them, in order to try a new path in the wood, when a far less agreeable visitor, Constantine, made his appearance. It was like a cloud coming over sunshine to the little girls when, bending over their basket now almost filed with flowers, they heard his unwelcome step.

"Oh! you've a basket—just what I want," said he; "there are lots of blackberries here. I'm going to gather a great many, but I've nothing to put them all into."

"Oh!—but my flowers—they are for mamma—pray, pray leave it alone!" cried poor Bertha, as his rude hand was laid on her basket.

"Trumpery and trash!" exclaimed the petulant boy, making a scatter of the flowers as he raised it.

"It's Bertha's basket, not yours!" cried the indignant Laura; "if Aleck were here, you would not dare"—

"Not dare!" he exclaimed, seizing her roughly by the shoulder.

"You shall not hurt my little sister," cried Bertha, catching hold of his arm.

Constantine shook her off with such violence that she fell and struck her head against a large stone, a blow which produced for some moments sharp pain, though not drawing any blood. Bertha began to cry.

"Baby that you are, there's nothing to whine about!" cried Constantine, who, between the mortifications of the drive, and his self-reproach for his own ungenerous and cowardly conduct, was now in extremely bad humour. Discontented with himself, he was so with all the world; for his pride, preventing him from owning the real regret which he felt, led him further and further into wrong; so he walked away now with a heart full of bitterness, much more to be pitied than the child to whom he had offered such unprovoked unkindness.

"Bertie, darling Bertie, don't cry, please don't!" exclaimed Laura, herself almost in tears; "I hope that it doesn't pain you much, does it, dear, dear Bertie?"

"Not so much now; just at first, dear," replied Bertha, stooping to kiss her little sister fondly, and hastily wiping her own eyes. "Oh, what a bad, bad boy he is! I do dislike him with all my heart!" cried Laura, clenching her little hand, and looking very indignantly after Constantine.

"I wish I were strong enough to beat him!"

"Mamma would say that we showed ourselves much stronger in forgiving him. We must not be overcome by evil, dear Lautie; remember what papa preached in his sermon."

"If Con only said that he was sorry"—

"We must make him feel sorry, whether he says that he is so, or not. You know in what way we can do that—how Fides threw down Benefits on his foes."

"Are you not angry with him, Bertie?"

"Yes; I can't help being a little, but I am struggling against the anger. I felt much worse after he had hurt our dear Aleck. It is easier to forgive unkindness to one's self. And, after all, Con has seemed improved lately; perhaps he has been trying to clamber out of the pit."

"He has fallen down then to the bottom, to *the very bottom*," repeated Laura, with emphasis.

"Then how vexed he must feel, when he had got up a little way! We all know how hard it is to climb, with Giant Selfishness at the top always trying to push us down again. But now, darling, help me to pick up these poor flowers; we cannot carry them so well as in the basket, but still we may tie them up in nosegays, and make a crown yet for mamma."

A very sweet feeling came over the spirit of little Bertha; perhaps Conscience was smiling upon her, perhaps she was feeling the soft balm of the tree of Forgiveness destroying the effects of the warm fount of Anger. Bertha and Laura were busy collecting the scattered blossoms, when they were startled by Adolphus running suddenly towards them, excitement in his manner, alarm on his face.

"Oh—come, come!" he breathlessly cried; "poor fellow, I fear that he has knocked out his eye!"

Both the girls uttered an exclamation of horror. "Aleck — is it Aleck?" cried Bertha, clasping her hands.

"No, no; it is poor Con," said the panting bay. "He was gathering blackberries, and he pushed aside the bough of a tree, and it started back and struck him just on the eye. You never saw what a way he is in!"

Bertha and Laura, guided by Adolphus, quickly hastened to the spot, where they found Constantine stamping with pain, and holding to his eye a handkerchief stained with blood. His cry of anguish had brought Aleck, who happened to be near. Pity now quenched the last spark of anger in the breasts of the Robys.

"Oh dear!—oh dear!—if he should be blinded!" exclaimed Laura.

"Do you know if the eye itself is hurt?" said Bertha anxiously to her brother.

"I do not know—he will let no one touch it. We had better put him into the chaise directly, and drive him to the doctor's; it is all on our way home."

"Quick, quick; let us go!" cried Bertha; and, neglectful of flowers, basket, blackberries, and everything else, the children hurried into the chaise. Constantine doubled himself up in the backseat, rocking himself backwards and forwards, and sometimes uttering a moan; Bertha watched him with

The Accident

pitying eyes; Laura's murmur, "Poor Con! poor Con!" were the only words uttered, while Aleck urged on Dobbin to such a pace as quite astonished Adolphus.

Happily they found the doctor at home, who immediately examined the sufferer. Constantine could hardly endure to remove the handkerchief, and expose his streaming eye to the light. It was too true that the blow had injured the eyeball itself, though the doctor hoped that the hurt was only of a temporary nature, and that if Constantine were kept for some time in a darkened room, and such remedies applied as were required, he might entirely recover the use of his eye, and not a trace of the accident remain.

This was a comfort, but poor Constantine appeared as though he could receive no comfort. As again, with bandaged eye, he returned to the chaise, he looked so pale, so unhappy, in such pain, that it was with a manner almost as tender as it would have been towards Aleck, that Bertha made his seat as comfortable for him as she could.

More trouble awaited the party on their return to Dove's Nest. Mr. Roby met them at the green door with the news that his wife had been suddenly called to attend her father, who had been taken dangerously ill with a fit. She had hurried away in the farmer's cart, for no other conveyance could at once be procured, to be in time for the next train starting for London. Many a fond message she had left for her children, as she departed with a very heavy heart, scarcely hoping to find her dear parent alive.

"It is very, very difficult to feel that all things are for the best," said Aleck to Bertha, as they retired from his room, after shutting the shutters for Constantine, and leaving him to try to get a little sleep after the suffering and fright which he had undergone.

"Grandpapa may recover," suggested Bertha.

"I trust that he will; but what a time we shall have of it while mamma is away! The doctor says that Con must be kept in a dark room and on low diet for a fortnight; how is he likely to stand that, he who can never bear for his will to be crossed for a moment! It seems as if troubles were coming so thick upon us."

"And yet we may be sure that it is for the best," said Bertha, softly. "We must believe that now; perhaps one day we may know it."

CHAPTER 11

THE PRISONER OF DARKNESS

A ll for the best!—yes, doubtless it is so," thought Aleck, as he watched the conduct of Bertha during that long, tedious fortnight. It seemed as if the necessity of thinking for others, of working for others, and at the same time fighting against besetting sins, had made the little girl several years older in that short space of time. Aleck had looked upon Bertha, before the arrival of the Probyns, as a nice little playmate, very willing to oblige him, and, though possessing a temper by no means perfect, very seldom letting him suffer from it. He had liked her then, he now respected her. He had felt her then inferior to himself; not only far below him in powers of mind, but with a disposition naturally less sweet, and an inclination to indolence, which prevented her from making the best of what abilities she had. Now he regarded his sister in quite another light; and if the Probyns had improved Aleck in outward behaviour, by obliging him to be careful of his words, and to avoid all vanity and affectation of manner, which exposed him to their ridicule, Bertha was influencing him by her example in another way, for the observant boy could not help feeling that in the Christian fight his sister was the firmer champion of the two. As the rice-plant is said to grow with wonderful rapidity in the rainy season, that it may keep its head ever above the waters rising around it, so the troubles and difficulties that beset her made the character of Bertha rise.

There were so many little things for her to do in the absence of her mother, that Bertha felt as though she never could manage them all. Thus the first foe which she had to overcome was Sloth; and the child rose an hour earlier than usual, that she might write to her mother and attend to her father's comforts without encroaching on other duties. She knew that her own lessons and Laura's should be learned; she set the latter her little tasks, and cheerfully undertook the tiresome business of teaching, though Laura, lively, playful, seldom giving her attention, was a pupil to try the patience of a much older instructress.

Then Constantine, poor unhappy Constantine, shut up in darkness and fed on beef-tea, became Bertha's peculiar charge. Adolphus took care to avoid going near him when he could help it;—"He is as peevish as a porcupine!" said he. But Bertha, as though all his rudeness and unkindness were forgotten, gave much of her time to beguiling the weary days of the poor prisoner. She altered her own study time and Laura's—at no small sacrifice of her convenience—that when Aleck and Pro were at lessons with Mr. Roby, Constantine might not be left alone. She chatted with him cheerfully, told him stories that she had heard, sang to him songs that her

Bertha's Attention to "Con"

mother had taught her, and sitting close to the window to make the most of the little light which struggled in, read to him till both eyes and voice were tired.

By this arrangement Bertha lost much of Aleck's society; she had to learn lessons when he was free to play, and sadly disinclined was she often to study, and perhaps even more so to teach, when already weary with amusing Constantine, and longing for a merry game with her brother. But Bertha's earnest prayer when she rose in the morning was that she might be enabled to fulfill the duties of the day; and each night, as she laid her tired head on the pillow, she felt thankful for the help that had been granted her. Angels look with more pleasure upon the efforts of a little child to overcome temptation and to serve her heavenly King, than upon the proud trophies of earthly conquest, the deeds of daring of earthly heroes.

And how felt Constantine during this long fortnight? Had his accident been to him all for the best? It was so, for he was thus given time to reflect, his mind was forced back upon itself; he might do wrong still, but he no longer could do so thoughtlessly. He was struck by the difference between the behaviour of the Robys and that of his brother towards himself. The latter shunned, the former sought his society; and no self-love could blind Constantine to the fact that it could be from no pleasure that they found in it. Why did Bertha never reproach him with the past?—why did Aleck employ all the resources of his fine memory to amuse one who had treated him with insult? Were they not showering down Benefits from the tree of Forgiveness?—was he not standing like one of the savages at the foot of it, looking up? for he could not avoid looking up at those whose conduct raised them above him. This was a grating reflection to Constantine, but he could not drive it from his mind.

Did he feel grateful? Perhaps he felt grateful; but if so, something prevented him from showing that he did so. He did not like to fancy himself indebted to anyone; the idea made him irritable and peevish. Then, when his heart reproached him for rude words to the kind girl who never returned them — who was leaving the sunshine and flowers that she loved, to sit in a gloomy apartment with him—Constantine had an uneasy remembrance of what had been read about Gratitude being chased into the swamp of Forgetfulness. He did not choose to examine his own heart sufficiently to ascertain whether anything like this could be the case with himself, but he felt somehow or other discontented with his own conduct—he began to suspect that there was something wrong in his character; Conscience was awake, and making her voice heard.

One day Aleck entered the room where Constantine was sitting gloomy and thoughtful, scarcely listening to the book which the patient Bertha had been reading to him for more than an hour.

"Good news!" he exclaimed; "another letter from mamma! The best account of grandpapa which we have yet had! The doctors say that he is now quite out of danger, and mamma feels so much happier about him, that she hopes to be here the day after tomorrow."

Bertha clapped her hands with an exclamation of pleasure; and Laura, who was playing with her doll in a corner,

Good News

jumped about the room in delight.

"Mamma's coming back!—mamma's coming back!" she cried. "Oh, she will have been a whole fortnight away! It has been like a year—I have missed her so!"

"I wonder," thought Constantine, "if I were to go away, if anyone would be sorry, or miss me." The answer which Conscience returned clouded his brow with a frown, which to the Robys, who knew not its cause, seemed like an unkind refusal to share in their joy.

"Bertha," said Aleck, "papa has given me leave to walk over to the farm to order a cream-cheese for mamma. The weather is so delightful to-day, and the walk is so pleasant over the fields, would not you like to come with me?"

"Very much; but I have all my lessons to learn, and to hear Laura the multiplication-table."

"Not done them yet—how's that! They used to be all over by this hour. Why, what have you been about all the morning?"

Bertha glanced at the book which lay on her knee, and then at Constantine, who felt her silence more than he would have done any words.

"I might make some trifling return," thought he, "I might offer to hear little Laura, but," Ah, what was the feeling that prompted that but?—the same which tried to stifle all emotions of gratitude, the same which made Constantine ashamed to own that he knew that he had behaved ill towards those who repaid all his insolence with considerate kindness.

"I will take the multiplication-table in hand," said Aleck, gaily, "and the spelling lesson besides. Here, Lautie pet, put down your doll, and look like a sober little student, and tell me if twice two makes three. Don't hurry with your own lessons, Bertie dear; I'll wait for you—we shall have plenty of time for our walk."

Constantine's opportunity was lost, and he felt more angry with himself than ever.

The next day the doctor paid Dove's Nest a visit, looked at the injured eye, and declared it to have so far recovered from the blow, that though reading and writing were to be avoided for the present, Constantine need no longer be considered as a prisoner. The look of honest pleasure and sympathy on the faces of the Robys touched him more than he would have chosen to own; he felt for a moment inclined to thank them for their kindness, then, as if a seal were on his lips, he pressed them together and was silent.

But Constantine and his brother could not avoid being participators in the pleasure with which Mrs. Roby was welcomed back on her return. They shared with her children in making the garland which was suspended over the entrance of Dove's Nest; they crowded with them to the green door when the sound of wheels was heard; and though Laura had the first kiss, and Bertha the first smile, while Aleck's hand was pressed in his mother's, the Probyns were not forgotten at the moment of arrival; and in the little remembrances which she had brought from London, Mrs. Roby made them share alike with her children. Kind inquiries after Constantine's eye were uttered in the same tone of affectionate interest as they might have been spoken by his mother. Oh, how much was there to tell, and how much to hear on the first evening of Mrs. Roby's arrival!

If one of the party was more happy than all the rest, it was Bertha: her young heart was bounding with delight! It was not only that she could again rest her head on that kind bosom, kiss that dear hand, and listen to the voice that she loved; it was a consciousness that her own affection had been tried and proved—that her mother would find that work had been done, and duties performed, as carefully in her absence as though she had always been near—that her mother would feel that her child was to be trusted, that she had indeed done her best to be a comfort to her parents.

"Now for the Giant-killer!" exclaimed Laura the next day, as, seating herself on Mrs. Roby's knee at the usual reading hour, she watched the opening of the well known volume.

"Had you time to prepare another chapter for us, mother, in the midst of all your anxieties?" said Aleck.

"One more chapter, my boy, and the last."

"The last!" exclaimed everyone in the room.

"Why, we have not half done with giants," cried Aleck; "I could name a dozen more at least. There's Stupidity"—

"Self-conceit," cried Adolphus.

"Cruelty," joined in Bertha.

"Disobedience," added Laura.

"Yes, my children, there are many more giants to be slain; but I think that my tale has explained to you sufficiently the nature of our fight, and of the enemies to be subdued, to enable you to find them out for yourselves. Let each search his own heart carefully—our hearts are our chief battle-ground—and having discovered what sins most easily beset him, let him apply himself resolutely, with watchfulness and prayer, to overcome the evil principle within."

"To-morrow is Sunday," observed Aleck; "I have just been thinking of something to vary the holy occupations of the evening. Suppose that we all sit round the table as we are doing now, each with a pencil and paper; you will give out the name of some enemy, and we will write down examples from Bible history of those who conquered, and those who were conquered by it; then we will give in our papers to you, and they will be read aloud in the hearing of all."

"Not a bad idea," replied Mrs. Roby.

"But I can't write," suggested little Laura.

"You shall think, then, without writing," said her mother, "and tell us upon what characters you have fixed, before any of the papers are read."

"I know what I should write if Hate were the enemy named," cried Adolphus; "King Saul was overcome by it quite!"

"And who conquered the evil passion?" inquired Mrs. Roby.

"David; at the cave of Adullam!" replied Aleck.

"Several examples might given," said his mother; "we will certainly try your new Sunday recreation tomorrow. And now to proceed with my tale."

CHAPTER 12

GIANT PRIDE

Fides rested for some hours that night in a small hut by the wayside, which he found deserted and empty. He awoke in the morning refreshed, and, girding on his sword anew, set out in search of Experience. He walked on for some time without meeting with any adventure, until he judged that he must be near the forge; but before proceeding further he sat down near a small stream, which flowed brightly over pebbles and sand, reflecting the emerald moss that clothed its banks, and the willows that bent over its waters. Here Fides laved his hands and his face, and stretching himself full-length on the turf, enjoyed the stillness of the scene.

"A fair sky above, a goodly carpet below, and pleasant meditations for thy companions! Thou hast well chosen thy place of repose, brave champion, and well earned thy moments of rest!" said the voice of someone behind him.

Fides lifted up his eyes and beheld near him a tall stately figure, clad like himself in the armour of a knight, but bearing, instead of a sword, a massive crooked staff, which appeared to be made of some dark heavy metal.

"Dost thou come as friend or foe?" exclaimed Fides, springing up, and instinctively laying his hand on the hilt of his sword.

"I am a friend to all gallant spirits like thee."

"And a servant of my King?"

"At least the enemy of those who are his foes," replied the stranger knight, evading the question. He threw himself carelessly down on the turf, but Fides, whose mind was not quite satisfied yet, remained standing until his further inquiries were answered. "Thou hast not a sword!"

"I have left it at home—none can use it more skilfully than I; but in its place I at present carry this weighty staff, which I have found at least equally successful in slaying the

The Strange Knight

giants whom I have encountered;" and as he raised his strong arm, and shook the staff on high, a deadly weapon it appeared in his hand.

"What giants hast thou slain?" inquired Fides, with a growing respect for his companion.

"I crushed Meanness with one blow of my staff—he never spake a single word after; I drove Gluttony to hide in caves and holes; I penetrated the strong fort of Avarice, and forced him to yield up some of his treasures; I killed Cowardice, and cut off his head; and, in short, I believe that the good cause never found a champion less ready to flinch from its defence."

"And thy name, brave knight?" said Fides, now seating himself beside him without misgiving.

"My name is High-Spirit; I am of ancient family; I am connected with the noblest in the land!"

All this time the stranger had been speaking in the language of the country of Fides; there was something, perhaps, a little peculiar in his pronunciation, something that was like the accent of a foreigner, not of a native, but still he spake fluently and well, and Fides rejoiced to think that he had been joined by a comrade so valiant.

"I have heard of thy exploits," continued the stranger knight, "and have mightily triumphed in thy success. Thou wert not the first to attack Giant Untruth; he was once sorely wounded by me, and how he escaped alive, I wot not!"

"Not, I trust, by thy holding parley with the foe?"

"Holding parley with Untruth!" exclaimed the knight, turning round fiercely; "I would dash out the brains of any one who dared but to hint such a thing!"

Words such as these sounded strange in the ears of Fides; in their proud boldness they were so unlike the language wont to be spoken by the servants of the King, that the warning of Gratitude flashed across his mind, and he drew himself a little further off from his comrade.

"Thy arm is mighty, thy hand strong," Fides said aloud, "but the power given to us is not to be employed in avenging any insult to ourselves."

"The power given to us!" repeated the knight, with a scornful smile; "the strength with which I fight is my own, and," he added, firmly grasping his heavy staff, "I use it when, and against whom I please!"

"I do misdoubt thee sorely!" cried Fides, springing to his feet; "me thinks thou art little like a champion of the Truth; how shall I know thee for one?"

"Speak I not in thine own tongue?" said the stranger, also rising, but more slowly, from the earth; "thou art strangely suspicious, my comrade!"

"Can'st thou read this?" cried Fides, rapidly drawing with his sheathed sword a few words on a spot where some white sand had been left by the receding of the river.

"I repent—I am grateful"—such were the brief sentences hastily traced by Fides, the first that came into his mind. He pointed to the writing with his sword, and turning his steady gaze upon the stranger, repeated his question, "Can'st thou read this?"

The false knight scarcely glanced at the words which he knew that he never could master; with a glare like a tiger's ere he springs, whirling his mighty staff round his head, he uttered but the exclamation, "Ha! thou knowest me!" and rushed in his fury to the attack.

Oh, who has not felt the fearful strength of Pride, who now engaged in deadly conflict with Fides! Never had the champion been more sorely beset, never had he more felt the need of help! Even his good sword seemed scarcely to avail him here; the giant, who had suddenly risen to his formidable height as soon as his real nature was discovered, parried every blow aimed at him so well, showered down his own with such rapidity and strength, that foot by foot Fides gave way before him! Strong indeed is the weapon of the Will, few are there upon earth who can withstand it! One crushing stroke fell upon the helmet of Fides; it gave not way, that

The Fight with Giant Pride

covering of well-tempered steel, but the knight reeled and staggered with the blow; sparks seemed to fly from his eyes; he could scarcely see the enemy before him; for an instant he was blinded by Pride, and scarcely conscious of anything but the faint cry of Conscience as she fled to seek aid for her champion.

Down came another blow upon Fides' right arm. It dropped numb—the sword fell from his grasp. The giant, foaming with rage, pressed on his advantage; he dashed his fainting adversary to the ground, and raised his heavy staff to destroy him. At that moment—that terrible moment—when all appeared lost forever, a stone thrown from some unseen hand struck the strong arm which was raised to smite. Pride started at the unexpected blow, and for an instant let fall his staff and glanced round to see who was his new assailant. Precious opportunity that might never come again! Fides with his left hand seized the dangerous weapon, and even as he lay on the ground, struck the foot of Pride with all the force that he could muster. Yet little impression made that blow on the giant; it rather served to stir up his rage than to wound him: he stopped, not to wrest the Will from Fides, as at that time he might easily have done, but to make himself master of the knight's good sword, which lay bright and glittering on the turf.

But the wondrous weapon was not one which could be wielded by the unholy hand of Pride; the golden hilt which Fides had rested on so often, burnt the hand of the enemy of his King, as though it had been formed of red-hot iron. With a cry of pain the giant dropped it from his hold, and the next moment it shone in the grasp of Fides.

Yes, the champion of the Truth was again on his feet, wounded, weary, but full of courage and hope. The painful struggle was coming to a close; thrice and again he struck boldly at Pride, and oh, the joy, the relief, when at last the most dangerous of his foes bit the dust!

Every muscle quivering with the efforts which he had made, breathless, gasping, scarcely believing his own success, Fides stood by the lifeless form of the giant, leaning on his own faithful sword!

And now he was approached by an old man with silvery hair and a long white beard, but a form still strong and unbent, and a face whose furrows had been made rather by thought than time. It was Experience himself who, in the hour of need, had come to the assistance of the knight, and who had flung that stone which, at a critical moment, had diverted the attention of the giant.

Warm was the gratitude of Fides, though his faltering tongue had scarcely power to express it. Experience, with kindly pity for the suffering knight, invited him to his dwelling, which was near, where rest and refreshment might be found, and where his wounds would be skilfully dressed.

"And oh, leave not that behind, noble knight!" cried Experience, pointing to the dark, crooked staff of the Will, which lay near the dead body of Pride; "take it, it once belonged to thy King; it is precious when devoted to him, it is the noblest fruit of thy triumph to be able to lay it at his feet."

Fides obeyed, and with feeble steps followed his new guide, whose manner, though grave, and almost stern, yet inspired him with confidence and respect.

The dwelling of Experience was on a hill, which commanded a wide prospect around. Part of it was divided from the rest, where a glowing furnace, an anvil, and various tools hung around, sufficiently showed the occupation of its possessor.

The Old Man

Balm was poured into the bleeding wounds of Fides; wine was given to sustain his fainting strength; the mist before his eyes cleared away, he felt himself reviving again.

"Oh, Experience," he said, as he laid his hand on the Will, "how can this instrument, once used by Pride, be ever an acceptable offering to my King?"

Experience took from a small casket a phial labelled "Submission," which contained a colourless fluid. He poured a few drops upon the dark heavy metal, then rubbed the staff with a rough hairy cloth, and wherever the liquid had touched, there was a spot of bright glittering gold!

"This rough cloth is Discipline," said the old man; "with patience, through its rubbing thou shalt see all the value of the Will when restored to its rightful owner."

"Yet can I not offer to my king that which is crooked and bent! It bears too evident tokens of having been in the service of Pride!" And as Fides spake, he tried and tried again with all his might to straighten the massive staff, but the tough metal resisted all his efforts!"

"The Will is crooked indeed, but it may be straightened," said Experience; "we have other ways of working. My furnace of Affliction is near." So saying, before Fides had time to reply, he plunged the staff into the red glowing fire.

"Give it back!" exclaimed the knight, with impatience; "anyway, anyway but this."

"No way but this," said the old man, firmly, keeping back the hand that would have snatched it from the fire. "See how the gold is brightening, see how the metal is softening in the furnace. Submit the Will to what is needful to make it perfect, a precious offering, acceptable and pure."

So saying, Experience drew it from the furnace of Affliction, and laid it on the anvil of Trial. He struck it with his heavy iron hammer, but was interrupted by Fides.

"No more—thou wilt destroy it; no more—it is enough!"

"Not yet," replied the old man, and struck it again.

"Stay thy hand!" exclaimed Fides; "it can bear no more."

"Yet a little patience," cried Experience, and struck was it again. Then the Will was restored to Fides—straight, pure, beautified; oh, how unlike that staff which had been so deadly in the grasp of Pride!

As Fides stood gazing on the fair gift before him, once more, and for the last time, the shining robe and star-wreath of Conscience flashed on his sight. Never before had her smile been so glad, so beaming with the radiance of Heaven.

"The work is done—the fight is over!" she exclaimed;

The Forge

"thou art summoned to the presence of thy King! A messenger is even now waiting to conduct thee to the home which thou so long hast desired! Go, bearing with thee the offering of a conquered Will, the acknowledgment that not even that should be thine own, and the remembrance of foes bravely met and overcome, through the might of Him who armed thee for the fight! Go in humility, go in joy, confiding in the love which hath preserved thee through temptation, and never will leave thee nor forsake thee; go where all is gladness, rejoicing and peace—where war and danger shall be known no more!"

"How glad—oh, how glad he must have been!" cried Laura, "to be called to his King, and wear the crown, and be so happy, and never, never have such fighting again! The messenger must have been very welcome."

"The messenger must have been Death," observed Aleck, gravely; "he alone puts an end to that war."

"I scarcely understood that last part about the Will," said Bertha, in a hesitating tone.

"I think that, young as they are," replied Mrs. Roby, "my children have already had some experience of the power and peril of a strong will which is under the command of Pride. To submit that will in all things to the Lord, is the highest exercise of Christian faith and love; and as we are unable of ourselves to change our proud and stubborn wills, trials and afflictions are often sent to soften our hearts, and purify our affections."

Constantine, who had been a far more attentive listener than he had ever appeared before, remained for some moments in deep thought, resting his brow on his hand. What was passing through his mind it is not needful to inquire, but when at length he raised his head, he said, "What were those words by which Pride was found out, those words which he could not master?"

"I repent— I am grateful," replied Adolphus; "ah, Pride could never be brought to say that!"

"Then what was the last victory of Fides, must be my first," said Constantine, rising from his seat; and flushing up to his temples with the effort which he was making, he held out one hand to Aleck and the other to Bertha, and pronounced firmly, as if determined to overcome the resistance of the giant in his own heart, "I repent of my conduct to you; I am grateful for your kindness; I hope by the future to make up for the past!"

Great was the astonishment of the children at a victory so sudden and unexpected, where they had not even been aware that any conflict was going on. Warmly, joyfully, Aleck and Bertha pressed the offered hand—Adolphus laughed, but not in derision—Laura looked up with innocent wonder at the "bad, bad boy," standing the conqueror of Pride, like Fides. But a tear stood in the eye of her mother; there was mingled prayer and thanksgiving in her heart: thanksgiving—that the Holy War had at length been commenced; prayer—that it might end in triumph everlasting!

Dear readers, have you known anything of this War— have you ever drawn the sword of Fides, or fought with the enemies of your king? Have you broken through the web of Sloth, struggled out of the pit of Selfishness, choked up the fount of Anger, and resolutely thrown aside "bitter words" as unworthy the use of a Christian? Have you overcome the feeling of Hate, and striven with Benefits to subdue those who have wronged you? Have you pursued Untruth even into his most secret lurking-place, and never stained your lips with a falsehood? Have you tried to conquer your own proud rebellious spirit, and, submitting your Will in all things to your Lord, made His service your delight, His glory your aim? Perhaps you never till now thought of looking upon life as the battle-field of the Christian; you knew not that your own hearts were full of foes that you could not conquer in strength of your own. Oh, then, if it be for the first time, ask, ask fervently for that grace which can overcome all; hold fast your glorious sword—the Word of God; go forth with Conscience for your guide, and Prayer for your safeguard. And oh, may He who alone can give you the victory make you more than conquerors here, and crown you with immortality in the eternal mansions which He has prepared for those who love Him!